Lyrical Love Lines
Of
Yours and Mine

By: Roger Smith

 www.trafford.com

North America & international
toll-free: 1 888 232 4444 (USA & Canada)
fax: 812 355 4082

Contents

Love

Problems

Passion

Love

Feelings Shown
Are Feelings Known

By spontaneously buying you flowers, gifts and rings, it don't necessarily mean that I am trying to cover up after doing wrong things; I am just showing you the appreciation of you being my woman and the happiness it brings. Every time that I come to you to hug, kiss you or sing, it don't necessarily mean that I especially want something, my heart was aching or I am trying to cover up after being on a wild fling; I am just showing the joy of having you, as my queen, and me, your king. I don't have time for no lying, cheating, disrespecting, playing, hating, not giving but always taking and not appreciating; I would be making a bomb that is just waiting for detonating. I don't want that bomb to backfire on me and blow up in my face; I would then be there just looking so stuck on stupid with my mind blown and lost in space. I want to really get to know your beautiful, intelligent and strong heart and mind more and not concentrate solely on your body; I want to get to know you better as a person and never a sex object because you really are somebody. If I didn't get to know you for you and was only caught up on *sex*, when the sex gets old or later on in life after you go through menopause and I become impotent, then what are we supposed to do *next*? Sleep restlessly, without each other, then *wake up*? *Make up* to later *break up*? No, that would simply *take up*... too much *time*! Why should I mess things up now that you are already *mine*? I ask myself that question time after time and a logical answer I never do *find*. I have loved you for far too long to just let everything go without trying to make it right; we have invested far too much time and energy into each other so do you think that I actually would let you go without a good fight? Hell, *no*! I could never let you go and this I want you to always know; I love you from the crown of your head to the bottom of your toes and I won't just say it to you, baby, but I am going to let it show! Just thinking about losing you makes my heart drop to my knees and causes me to break out into a cold sweat; if I ever lost you, it would feel as if I had made, lost and can't cover a multi-million dollar bet. I never want our relationship to wither, dry and die so let's keep it soaking wet; while the sun is shining so beautifully and brightly in our relationship, I never want to see that sun set!

My Deepest Emotions

If you take a look into your heart and a journey through your *mind*, deep true emotions and sweet memories you may *find*. I have taken a look into my heart and mind and it urged me to think; despite all that I have or have had, there is still a missing link. Through all the good times, hard times, compromising and strife, you have became a big, important part of my life; therefore, I don't want you to just be my woman anymore but I'm asking that you become my wife. You are the golden apple of my eye and the candlestick of my heart; you are a big part of me in which I never want to part. The love, the pain, the joy, the sorrow and everything else that we have been through have only made our love that much stronger; all these things should make our love and passion for each other much more resilient as we stay together even longer. Longer and everlasting is what I want our love to be; higher than the sky and the stars and deeper than the deep, blue sea is still not enough to describe what your love means to me. Your love is like the blood that keeps running through my veins to help give me life and the strength to go on each day; it is like a good, dependable mother who makes a young child cry and be sad whenever she goes away. It is like a tree that is over a hundred years old and still seems young, strong and continues to grow; it is like the sun on a tropical island that keeps me hot with passion for you, so much that it never seems to get cold enough to snow. Therefore, I want to repay you with as much or more love as you has given me; your love has brought me out of the darkness and blindness of being with other no-good women, shining so brightly in my heart, so that a better relationship and outlook on life I can finally see. Before, I was blinded to the fact that a wonderful woman out there, like you, could be mine; like valuable treasure hidden in a pile of junk, damn, you were a good find! So, therefore, I want to give you a huge part of my life as God has given us the world; I really want to be your husband and for you to become my wife, because I am tired of you just being my girl. Your love is so warm and shines very brightly in me, brighter than the closest star, even the Sun; we are strongly in love with each other so, hopefully, now our love will make us inseparable and become perpetual as we become one. I know that sometimes we may get on each other's nerves and disagree; this I promise you though, not the good Lord above or the devil destined for hell below will never take the love that I have for you away from me. And I truly hope and pray that nothing ever comes along to take the love that you have for me away; your love has a good home in my heart and I want that love to always stay!

Maintaining Our Love

Infatuation and passion is never everlasting; therefore, your true love in my heart long term is what I'm asking. I want to make sure that our love stays strong and endure the test of time so that it would seem to be able to last forever; I can't wait and procrastinate to make our love for each other stronger so it's now or never. Because, if our love ever had gotten *weak* and we went our separate ways and didn't *speak*, it would cut deeply into my soul and slowly drain away my life until nothing would be able to control the *leak*. My heart would constantly be in *pain* until it infected my *brain* and then my sanity and logic would begin to *drain* until I couldn't *maintain*. I am just so crazy about you and no matter what you may say or do, I will always be true; I will always try my best to give my all, my one hundred percent or more, into the relationship but I can only speak for myself and not you. I am not asking that you be as strongly in love with me as I am for you, as long as you remain faithful and *true*. That would make me stick closer to you so that our bond would be much stronger and longer lasting than something held together by welding or super glue; if we ever gave up on our love for each other, I would feel a whole like sicker than if I had the worst type of flu and would give up on being my ethnic color because I would always stay blue. This relationship, I could never just let it go and easily give it all up; therefore, I will fill your heart, mind and body with more love and passion than you need constantly, like an overflowing cup. I have to always try to keep you happy and constantly be working to keep our love durable, fastidiously; I will instantaneously try to correct my mistakes, after doing things erroneously, and do things more fun and exciting things, spontaneously, and try not to ever do things, monotonously, but keep my feelings toward you strong and actions diverse, miscellaneously. I wouldn't give you just a small hug without following behind it with an even bigger kiss; I wouldn't allow you to always give me all that I want and desire, without also trying to fulfill your every wish. I wouldn't indulge in any desire for other women and devour those desires, like appetizers and melted butter with expensive filleted *fish,* because my love and passion for you will always be my only main *dish.* I will try to never neglect to keep myself in check; when it comes to working hard to keep us together, through any hard times and stormy weather in our lives, I have no problem at all with breaking a sweat. Enduring the pain and trials of our relationship and life will just help make our love stronger; loving you the same, whether you are around me or away, will only help make our relationship last that much longer. I will never intentionally do anything to hurt you or make our love for each other go weak; you will see for yourself of my love, respect and appreciation, instead of just reading or hearing it from the words that I may write or speak.

Fulfilling My Love

I want to please you, in both words and deeds; I never want to fall short in fulfilling both your desires and essentials so let me know what you want and need. If you get hungry for my love and passion, I'm going to let you *feed*. If you are hurt and scarred from past relationships or experiences in life and have emotional wounds that haven't quite healed, I will not reopen those wounds and let you bleed; if you want our relationship to grow and be stronger, I'll be the first to fertilize the soil and plant the seed. I can't continue to help it grow all alone because it takes two; I can't allow any negative emotions and experiences to tear apart our relationship and choke it to death like overgrown weeds or grow wild and menacing like undomesticated animals outside of a zoo. I love your heart, mind and body as if they were my own and I wouldn't waste my time and breath telling you if it wasn't true; therefore, I want to give you all the love, appreciation, respect and much more to keep our love and passion for each other continually jumping further and longer than fleas, locusts, frogs and kangaroos. Are you ready for all this? Is this what you have been waiting *for*? If so, I will do and give you all this and so much *more*! Come into my heart to stay because I have long ago opened the door; now you can shop and get many of the needs and wants that you may desire, as long as you are with me, like having a million dollar debit or food stamp card in a department or grocery store. Open up to me, fully, so that our love and passion may flow into each other as rapidly as sweat pours from pores;

I would never intentionally hurt you, physically or emotionally, to leave you sore. If our love is to never be dull and boring, let's keep it hardcore; I never want it to be concealed and quiet so let's keep it at a roar. Do I love you more than you love me?...Hell, I am not keeping *score*! Let us continue to work hard to always love, care for, respect, appreciate, be faithful, spontaneous, spend good, quality time with each other, etc. and never *rest*. If we continue to stay faithful and true to each other and never stray, our lives and relationship will always be blessed; if we continue to allow our love and passion to thrive and live freely and deeply in our hearts, they will never be broke or homeless!

Come And Get To
Know Me And My Love

Hello, baby girl! You are so beautiful and fine and your body is perfectly shaped, like a cello; seeing you strut your stuff like that, as Bill Crosby says in the commercials, "Give me some of that J-E-L-L-O!" I'm sorry, sweet lady, I am moving too quick; I have to be careful what I say so that my true feelings for you, that I say to you, will get inside your head and stick. I know that you are very fine but your body is not the only thing that I want from you; I need to get to know your heart and mind, first, so that they may feed and fill up my emotions and intellect, quickly, like the stomach being filled after eating cornbread mixed with beef stew. And you best believe I will give you a fill; I am not trying to talk game because what's the use of elaborating my feelings to you if I can't keep it real? Therefore, real is what I want our potential, future feelings for each other to always be; maybe, in the past, you had been blinded by fake and broken dreams from other men but I want you be able to see that if you ever get with me, I will detoxify, heal and protect your heart, mind and body from all the toxins, carcinogens and impurities that other men may had left in your emotions and mentality quicker than any medicine, multi-vitamins, home remedies or green tea. Whenever you want to see how great this thing will be, just give me the shovel and I'll plant and water the tree; a special place in my heart will be opened for only you because only you will possess the master key.

If you just give me the chance to know you, you would soon see that you will be my favorite subject and I'll study hard to obtain my master's degree; I will close my heart to other females and put up a sign that reads, "NO VACANCY!" I want to be your true friend before I become a lover because by first getting to really know one another, we stand a much better chance of not losing each other; I want us to be as close to each other's heart, as sister and brother. I want to be the one to get inside of your heart so that I can be there to hold it together, if you allow the players and other no-good men to tear it apart; if we really were meant to be, the latter times of our potential relationship will be as marvelous as the start. We should try to stick together and never grow apart; let us shape each other into the better person that we want each other to be and then show each other off to the world, as beautiful pieces of art. We would then be an epitome of what real love should always be; we would be much more sure of each other's love and how to please each other, instead of having to do things hypothetically or theoretically. I would never want our good qualities to change but stick with us for life; we have to endure through the present to ensure the future of us, hopefully, succeeding from being friends and then being in a relationship to maybe you becoming my lovely, wonderful wife.

Old Love

You was once a small, shapeless and unattractive female but now you are fully developed and full grown; I remember back when we were little kids, we used to hump on each other with our clothes on, not knowing what we were doing was wrong. But look at you now, looking all P-H-A-T or pretty, hot and tempting, all fine as can be; you should be a supermodel so why don't you get some practice in by modeling for me, personally? You can model skirts, shorts, dresses, bikinis, thongs or whatever, I don't care; looking all beautiful, with your sexy body and lovely face, along with your silky hair, it would be hard to keep from doing anything else but only stare. You went through school and college but you still seem to not quite believe in *yourself.* Instead of presenting yourself openly, to your fullest potential, why do you seem content with just sitting on a back shelf; why are you content with nickel and diming on these low paying jobs when you can use your knowledge to obtain so much more wealth? When everyone else was running the streets and in the clubs, you were satisfied with just staying at home, no doubt; I'm glad that you had a strong enough mind to not let the players, scrubs and thugs turn you out. (You are a strong, independent woman, that's what I'm talking *about!*) You are known throughout the community for your integrity, intelligence and skills; you always held steadfastly to your ambitions and values, to never become promiscuous, catch a disease and later fall ill. While you had always stayed true to positive priorities and put them first, many of our peers are locked up, strung out on bad habits or have already taken that ride in a hearse; I really hate to see so much drama, violence and ignorance continually destroying our lives, ambitions and potential, like a generational curse. Be not "the little engine that could" but be "the little engine that do"; if you just present yourself, your skills and talents for others to see, as I took notice, the right people to help you will take notice, too. I don't want to see you let go of your hopes and dreams but I want to see you succeed; maybe you can be the torch that help guide our peers and others out of the darkness of ignorance and lost hope if you only take the lead. You have such a beautiful heart, mind, body and soul; I could never allow you to keep being like a "diamond in the rough" and let you go undiscovered and untold because you are more precious to me than platinum and gold. I need a good woman like you on my team and by my side; if I had to choose and elect a female to rule and govern inside my heart, you would definitely win by a major landslide. We were once kids but now we are older; never be afraid to take a chance in life to better yourself so please be bolder!

We Must Never Allow
Our Relationship
To Grow Old And Cold

You look so radiant today, as always, baby, and your beautiful face seems to make your whole body glow; I just want to compliment your inner and outer beauty, just in case no one else lets you know. I know that you sometimes get stressed and tense so I want to give you a good, full body massage, from your head to your toes; you take such good care of that fine body and it really shows. Anytime that you start thinking and talking to me about how you are not as beautiful anymore, that part of the conversation we will have to close; I want you to always know that no matter how long we are together, I will always see you as a beautiful, freshly picked rose in which I never want to dispose. Your love and passion for me is something that I never want to lose; sometimes you may start thinking and feeling differently but you might as well stop looking for clues. Your sweet love and divine essence, I never will intentionally hurt and abuse; I know that all the gossipers, drama kings and queens can't wait to spread the news of a break up between us but, as long as I can help it, they might never hear the news. I want to always keep you around, no matter how old the relationship gets, because you have much more sentimental value to me than any of my old jewelry, cars, photos, pairs of pants and shoes; others may think that through disagreements and fights, it makes the relationship stronger, but to keep up mess and drama with you intentionally, I refuse. I will keep standing up as a man and treat you right, day and night, because as your man, that's my responsibility; you will never have to beseech me to work to try to pull the relationship back together and start acting right, if it should ever start falling apart, because I will actually do it willingly. Love, respect, trust, passion, faithfulness, appreciation, good quality time and positive communication with honesty are major parts of the whole key; if we started to lose even one of these qualities, the whole foundation of the relationship would sooner or later start to crumble, as you would see. I'm so glad that I've had the chance to experience, firsthand, how wonderful and exciting your love and passion can be; I can't afford to change and start acting strange to cause you to want to get away from my vicinity because I don't want no other man getting the best of your love and sweet passion but me. I'm not just going to give you the best of me also, but will give you my all with high definition and quality; what's the use and fun of staying with me, if I am going to only give you monotony and mediocrity? And you don't have to worry about me ever playing with your emotions and breaking your heart so that you will try to get back at me, vindictively; all the finer qualities you had been looking for in a man, you have found in me so now you don't have to keep looking for those things in another anymore and being so finicky. I have given you the truth and it set me free; to show and tell you how much I love and care for you, frequently, is my goal ultimately. I'm tired of referring to us as "you and I" but want to start referring to us as "we"; if you ever wondered how lovely a stable marriage could be, stick with me and it will become a strong possibility.

Needing Your Love

I want some dinner by candlelight and us walking and holding hands close and tight; by me, holding you firmly in my arms throughout the day and keeping you snugly against my body at night, with spending as much quality time with you, without giving in to infidelity and jealousy out of spite, it will allay many of the fusses and fights. I will sometimes, spontaneously, surprise and shower you with gifts and be a strong presence in your life, like a *monolith* because I really love and appreciate the woman that I'm *with*. I won't treat you differently around family and friends, ignore you or neglect to hold you and give you a kiss because sooner or later it will get you very pissed; I will try not to ever neglect to give you the love, appreciation, quality time and respect that you truly deserve, because if you ever had gotten fed up because of my wrongdoings and I be dismissed, everything you give me will surely be missed. It's not only about what you give me but what you mean to me; if you ever walked out of my life, because we are bonded like one, it will hurt and tear away a huge piece of me, you see? I would have no choice but to suffer through the pain and continually bleed; my emotional and mental being would then slowly deteriorate and die because having you reattached and bandaging me up would be all that I need. I would still be a weak and ill convalescent, paranoid from the notion that you might leave me again, so I would need your true love pumped back into me by an intravenous feed; I would also need your medicine of sexual healing with passion to help protect my coronary, bodily and mental essence, from the germs of negative emotions and outside problems waiting to grow and choke out my heart and mind's health like unkempt weeds. As long as I am physically and emotionally healthy, I will give my true love and passionate nourishment to you; through thick and thin, sickness and health, poverty and wealth, I know what I have to do to stay true. I love you from the bottom of my heart and want you to always know; you will always get the real deal of my love and sexual healing and never a placebo. I mostly want us to give each other the rare gift of unconditional love; no one will be able to take it away because it was placed in our hearts from God above.

Hooked On Your Love

I don't know what you do when you do what you be doing to me, baby girl; you have me twisted and my mind is still in a swirl. I could give you the best of my love also but I really don't think that you are ready; I would have you wrapped and twisted around me, tighter than a fork haves spaghetti. With our love intertwined, both yours and mine, I hope that only true love we shall find; we, being two of a kind and tangled in the web of each other's love, would never have us in a negative bind. The thought of you breaking away sends chills up my spine; it is a lot worse than having a big fish on the hook, getting it almost reeled in and then it snaps the line. You are a much bigger catch than I ever dreamed of or had ever been wishing; I'm so glad that I used the right bait when I went female fishing. Now that I have you hooked and reeled in, there is no way I am going to throw you back; you are a full course meal instead of just a one-piece snack! Before, I was so afraid that I had lost you because I had tried to hook you a little too late; don't have to worry now because I have you with your love and passion, hot and ready to devour, but I must first say grace before I clean and lick my plate. You can best believe that I will feed my love and passion back to you, too; for this thing to work, it has to be a little of "give" and not always "take", true? I know that it won't be a piece of cake but we must try our best to not make too many mistakes; I will keep trying to make sure our fortresses of love is built strong enough to endure the test of time, no matter how long that it may take. Anything valuable to us is always worth fighting for; if wrongful emotions and other negativity try to break into our hearts to destroy our love and passion, we have to make them get the hell out of our hearts, lock and bar the windows and deadbolt the door. We have to put on the helmet of faith to know, and never be unsure, insecure and untrusting of each other; we have to put on the body armor of devotion and have the shield of fidelity to help protect us from anything that will try to get into our hearts and minds and cause us to go into the arms of another. And we have to put on the shoes of unity to be able to see eye-to-eye and walk hand-in-hand; you are no better than me and I am no better than you and want you to be my only woman, as I am your only man, understand? We have to do whatever it takes to stay strong in each others' love because I truly care; we have to be careful not to become careless and weak-minded because there are other fishermen and fisherwomen after us out there.

Looking At Why
I Should Love You

Looking into your eyes, I immediately see an epiphany of what's inside me; so immaculate, clear, precious and pure is what I picture and always want my love for you to be. Not cloudy, miry or *impure* but unblemished, firm, certain, *mature* and *sure*. Into those eyes, I also see that you are innocent, unyielding, benign and wise; I don't see someone that is malevolent, malicious, immature, without knowing what she wants out of life, and full of lies. I also see someone that is wary, having experienced prior hurt and pain; I see someone that has cried a few to cleanse her soul from the hurt and pain and replenish it with love and joy, like the forest rebirthing and recuperating from a forest fire after long periods of sunshine and heavy rain. Therefore, I will never hurt you and cause you any pain because I have also experienced painful emotions so I know how they feel; I will always try to be truthful and real, hold, kiss and love you, fully, so that we both may heal. Then after we heal, I will continue to nurture your heart, mind, body and spirit with love, joy and peace so that we both may stay well; we should strive to never bring any more despair, problems and drama back into our lives, to never resurrect those things of the past, because what's the point of helping you recuperate from painful emotions and experiences if I am going to take you right back through hell? It is like saving a cat from a tree, just to throw it into the ocean to let it drown; it is like helping a duck recuperate, after being shot and wounded by hunters, just to wash off all its flotation oil off its feet and burning off all its feathers and down. I could never be that cruel to anything or anyone, especially you, because I am not that type of man; hurting and bringing you down will be like doing it to myself, since we see things eye-to-eye, neck-to-neck and go hand-in-hand. That's what I am trying to get the next man to understand is that having a good woman's love, desire, respect, appreciation and aide in life is much better than having over nine hundred and ninety-nine grand because money comes and goes and is expendable; I'd rather have those pure qualities from a woman because those things can be perpetual, indispensable and much more dependable. But those things also have to be protected, like delicate glass, inside of the safe of our hearts; although love is stronger than steel, if you neglect and/or abuse it yourself, it won't take much for it to shatter and fall apart. Therefore, I want to enjoy and cherish our love, to value it more than priceless gems, jewelry and art; I never want to see the end of the road of our wonderful relationship because it had such a beautiful start.

Love Me Or Leave Me

As one, I am so glad to be a part of your life and love because together we are a winning team; I don't want to be a statistic of baby mama dramas, painful divorces, infidelity, domestic violence and other problems added with broken dreams. I also realize that our lives and relationship won't always seem like a "bed of roses" and "peaches and cream"; nevertheless, I never want us "faking it until we make it", pretending everything is much better than it seems. Working together, we shall stand, and divided, we shall inevitably fall; if we have to be together through always disagreeing, arguing, fighting, cheating, etc., what's the point of being together at all? Whatever you want from me that you haven't already gotten or have done, all you have to do is call; I will be more focused on giving you your "needs" than fulfilling your "wants" because you or no other female will have me like a dog chasing and retrieving a thrown ball. Sometimes, I might buy you a little something in the mall but always will be there to help pick you up if you ever should start falling; our love for each other have to be stronger than a steel wall, because our relationship will crash like a wet paper house with no problem at all if we wait to strengthen and repair it by procrastinating and stalling. It will be much harder to build back up, once it is down, because of much lost hope and trust; our relationship would be brittle and easier to break and crush, like crust. Therefore, maintaining a healthy and lasting relationship is a must; we can't afford to allow negative things in our life to build up and adhere in and on our hearts and minds, like corrosion and rust. If we are going to keep our relationship on the ground, go ahead and treat it like dirt and don't try to make it work; go ahead and go out places to mingle with other men and flirt. If we are going to act crazy like we are in a mental institution then go ahead and act a nut; sooner or later, I am going to get tired of all the sh.. and flush it all away, like the same stuff that comes straight out of my butt. That is definitely something I never want our relationship to come to; I really don't see it happening anytime soon as long as we keep it real and continue to stay true. Just continue to do all the right things as you've been doing and keep the love and passion in our lives percolating and brewing; let us focus on the present rather than past mistakes so that the present utopia in our lives we won't ruin. Nevertheless, we should really try to avoid committing the same wrongdoings again; it would be like continually asking God for forgiveness but be continually going out and committing the same sins. The place that we have for each other in our hearts won't only be a wonderful place to observe for only you and me; we will be an example for other people to observe and smile in approval, whenever they see.

Love Lines To Try
To Get You To Be Mine

Girl, you are a *hottie*! Your body's proportions is perfectly distributed, not a little but a lottie; if you want to go to my crib, I can get us back there laid back, chillin', but I wish that it could be as quickly as I can say, "Beam me up, Scotty!". We can chill there, lay back, watch some DVDs, drink a little bubbly and grub on anything in the house you prefer, but I think I'll have steamed vegetables, a potato and a steak they call the "T"; if you get a little tipsy, go to the bedroom and crash because you don't have to wait on me. I'll be there in about an half an hour after I shave and get out of the shower; if you are awake then, we can then have fun and party all night long because, as long I am enjoying myself with you, I'm not worried about wasted electricity/power. You must be a special girl to me because I don't try to get with just any female because I'm kind of selective; I really want to get to know you better but I am not going to ask you a lot of questions as if I'm a private detective. And I am not going to try to bomb rush you so there's no need to be nervous and, once we become closer, I won't be overprotective and demanding like the Secret Service; although, sometimes, I'm used to moving fast like the hare, I don't mind if you want to take it nice and slow, like the tortoise. I'm not saying that I want some of your good loving on the first date but after we get to know each other better, why procrastinate; after our feelings for each other grow stronger and we decide that we want to stay with each other longer, why should we worry about hurting each others' feelings or using each other only for sex, when the pain of broken hearts and other disappointments is something that maybe we can both relate? And if you are worrying about pregnancy, not potentially catching a disease or nasty infection, I will put some protection on my erection; I want to protect and secure my valuable and precious asset and dispose of all the other unworthy females out of my collection because that's why I made you my number one selection. So, why hurt you when I can be hurt myself; why try to build a relationship or something special with you if I am going to later destroy it and put it right to death? It might take a little while to make something really special out of this but, when it happens, it will be well worth the wait; whether we just be friends or go on to another level, our relationship we have to constantly regulate so that wonderful memories in the future we can both happily contemplate. I want to have and enjoy memories of us walking and holding hands, whether it's in the day or after dark, in the streets or in a park that is full of trees that's either full of snow or full of leaves; to love you and be affectionate the same, whether we are in private or in front of others, is something in which I truly believe. Even when I see you hanging out or if I am around my friends, I want to always be able to call your name, without shame, because I have nothing to hide, like other players trying to be with too many females and trying to run game; I never want to be trying to cheat and creep and sleep with other females because I would then make myself seem worthless to you and seem so lame. Therefore, I want to stay true, only to you, and pleasing each other, mentally and physically, is something that we can never hesitate to do; if we don't take the time to love and please each other, someone else will try to, so I never want us loving and later leaving each other without a clue.

Thank You For Staying True

I want to give you my sincere love, care, trust, respect and appreciation and, for all the things that you have done for me, I offer my gratification; for helping me change from being a player and womanizer into a devoted mate, I offer my congratulations. You helped me to look inside of myself and extract out all the negativity, hurt and pain; my heart was dry and withering from a drought of true love but you came along and brought on the rain. Having a female constantly showering me with real, true love is something that I am not really used to; you don't have to try very hard, because real love seems to just flow naturally from you. Therefore, I want to return as much or more love back to you as you have given me; you haven't seen anything yet of how sweet and real my love can be. I have no problem at all with putting my words into action; you may think that you have seen the most part of my love now but you have only seen a very small fraction. The love and passion that you have experienced so far is just the tip of the iceberg of the things to come and the things that I will do; even through the trials and tribulations of our relationship, I will always try to stay true. Although, I can't really prove it's destiny that you are together with me, I will just go with the flow, like the currents of the oceans or sea; on the other hand, we must condone and rectify when things go wrong, instead of just letting them be. Sometimes, it might take a struggle or mental fight to keep things right; negative emotions or circumstances might just rush upon us before they can be detected by our intuitive foresight. Nevertheless, our lives and relationship will be blessed if we work together in unity and don't allow stress to build up on our chest; until the day our relationship could handle the pressure of a nine-point-nine earthquake, I will and can not rest. If we ever stop having the love and strength to make things work, it makes no sense sticking around; if necessary, the same way I built a relationship up with you, I can build another one up from the ground. Hopefully, it will never come to that and be that way; if little, petty problems bring us down before we face much bigger ones, then I'm not sure we were meant to be together anyway. As long as our love and passion is strong and things are going so right, I never want to make them wrong; I am no greater than you as you are no better than me so let's sit, equally, high upon our thrones.

The Depth Of Our Love

With a million words, I still couldn't explain how deep my love for you is. In a million years, I still wouldn't be able to give you all the love and passion that I really want to give; your love for me is just so pure, true and real that everyday it gives me many reasons for wanting to live. My love for you is the same and has no intention to become lesser or negatively change; communication, honesty, respect, trust, appreciation and devotion are all just a few keys to keep us from concealing things and start acting strange. You are a very significant part of my life and I could never fully describe with words how much you really, truly mean to me; these feelings are much deeper, powerful and even more emotional than I ever would be able to tell you in poetry. But sometimes when I am off in a zone and want to be left alone, please don't think that I am neglecting you or your feelings and treating you wrong; my mind is not about gone but I just want to mellow out and release any negative emotions or problems out of my head that will eventually cause our relationship to not be as strong. No matter what you may say or do, I never want to take any problems or negativity that I may have on my mind out on you; my love for you will always stay true and I'll show you as often as I can and not only when we have foreplay, start to make love then screw. I will be there whether you are sick or healthy, richer or poorer, joyful or as you weep; I have no desire to cheat and creep because you are the only one that I want to make sweet love to so good that afterwards it puts you into a peaceful sleep so that you don't have to worry about tossing and turning, counting sheep. Rose petals in the bath tub, a sponge back scrub and an hour long, full-body massage with another good back rub will be some of the predecessors of our sessions of making love; wasn't having a man that treats you right, both day and night, one of the things that you always had dreamed of? Well, it don't have to be a dream anymore; you haven't seen all of my love yet because I have so much more for you in store. I know that all the love and passion that I will give you, you will adore; yes, it is much more than you had been looking for. I want to make love to your heart and mind before your body so that it may be more intense; if anyone says that they can fully sexually satisfy a woman, without any mental or physical foreplay at all, they will never, ever have me convinced. Pleasing you fully and not leaving you hanging makes much more sense; when you are completely allayed from all the problems and emotions that make you stressed and tense, you can focus more on the relationship so that it won't become so dull and dense. I'd rather enjoy our relationship with love and pleasure than dislike it with animosity, stress and pain; you have showered our relationship with so much love, pleasure, excitement and joy so continue to bring on the rain. It help eases any stress and pain that may affect my heart, body and brain; I know that it won't always be easy but a healthy relationship we must always strive to maintain.

Gracious, Senorita, I'm So Glad To Meet You

Que pasa, bonita senorita, I am so glad to meet 'cha; would you like to go out with me sometime and enjoy some **comida e` margaritas?** Oops! I apologize, sweet lady I am moving too fast; I just wanted to **andale** to try to get with you before someone as fine as you pass. I want to have a type of relationship that will last and is not just after a piece of that **trascero**; I just want to take it nice and slow and be a **cabellerro** to make a good impression so that I won't seem like a **grosero,** but what do you expect me to do besides trying to rush and be with a beautiful lady like you because I am certainly not **joto.** How far would it go between us? Who *knows?* All I want is at least for us to be able to leave each other saying, **"Mucho *gusto!*"** But if we ever became closer, I want to be able to tell you, **"Te quiro mucho!"** and really, truly mean it; if anyone should ask if we have ate at a **nuevo restaurante** or been to the **cine** to see some **nueva pelicula,** I want us to be able to tell them that, together, we've already ate there or have been there to already have seen it. I really would like to see the day when we are walking and holding **manos** and making future **planos,** realizing that I would want you to be my only **mujer** and, hopefully, I would be your only **hombre**; I am telling you this from the bottom of my **corazon** because I am not a little **niño** so silly games I do not play. And why should we worry about what our **amigos, amigas, familia** and others may say; if you take care of yourself, pay your own bills and is an independent **mujer**, don't you pretty much do whatever you want to do anyway? All I want to do is get inside of your **corazon**, to be able to there to hold it together if you allow another **hombre** to come in, break it and tear it apart; if things go any further between us, why can't the **futuro** of a **possible'** relationship be as **marvavilloso** as the start? I want to get to know and **apreciar** your **corazon e' mente** before I get to know your **cuerpo**; I really want to get to know you as a **persona** and never a **sexo objetar** because I want you to be someone that's really special to me, you know? I have no **problema** treating you **fuera comer** and maybe buying **nuevo zapatos para tu' pies**; I have a thang for Latino women, I must confess. I will never change the way I feel or act toward you in front of my family and friends; I will always show you **mucho amor** from the **dias** until the **luz del dia** ends. You are so beautiful with your **bella ojos**, **sexy labios**, **sedoso pelo** and **manos** that is so beautiful as a pair; anyway that we can **trabajo** to have a successful life together, I would **trabajar** hard to help get us there!

Contemplating From The Present To The Past Of How We Made Our Love Last

From the time that I first met you, I knew that you was the one for me; you melted the ice and warmed the coldness from my heart by your beautiful smile and voice that's always filled with joy, constantly. I couldn't wait to get to know you better, just to be able to hold you, kiss you and show you how much I truly care; whatever we want to achieve out of our life and relationship, I will not stop working, neither would I be satisfied, until we both get there. Together, I believe that we can achieve whatever we want to, if we strive hard enough toward it and walk in unity; if we do sometimes disagree, we must compromise and start back working together, quickly, because it is much easier if "you and I" do things as "we", don't you agree? It won't always be easy, but as a team, I know that we can; I will always work hard with you to help us get what we need and want out of each other and life because that is my responsibility as a man. You are never any lesser or better than me, because we're equal, and I will never get any self-gratification or pleasure by calling you derogatory words other than your name and showing you disrespect; you are my queen, my precious jewel and the only love of my life, so to loving you, caring, sharing, appreciating and spending good quality time with you, those things I can never neglect. If you don't know by now, I'm going to tell you so that you can be sure; we have put too much time and energy into the relationship to allow it to become a failure so let's continue to be civilized and act mature. The prospect of marriage, with you, no longer seems so uncertain and scary; we have loved each other too long and our love and passion for each other has really grown too strongly for us to allow our relationship to die and be put into an obituary and later buried inside of a cemetary. I remember back when we used to disagree and it later led into a *fight* but we always made up and were making sweet love before the end of the *night,* way before until sometimes after *daylight.* Sometimes, we had it hard and disappointments and much stress on our chest was all we seemed to feel; just when we thought that we had it easy and was about to get ahead, along came a mailbox full of bills. Quality times were good times; every moment that I shared with you made me proud and happy that you were all mine. All the *wining* and *dining,* traveling and going to fun places and laughing at good times with each other, until we were *crying,* was so special to me that I had no problem at all *buying.* And, most of all, we had no problem with saying to each other, "I love you!"; although we may had glanced briefly at other people we thought was cute and fine, to each other, we always had stayed true. Now that we have came a long way, from an uncertain past, I'm so glad that we have what it takes to make a wonderful relationship last; I would be more willing to mold each other and be conformed into the better person that we want each other to be, if later we are not going to shatter it all like glass. We have lasted and withstood the test of time for this long, so let's try to make it last even longer; by sticking with each other through thick and thin, and enduring through those hard times, it will make our relationship even stronger because we can't afford to allow our relationship and life together to ever become a goner.

I Can Never Get
You Out Of My Head

I try to go about my day concentrating on my tasks, but I can't seem to focus; you always, magically, pop up right in my head, like hocus pocus. I don't know what you do when you do the things that you do to keep me loving you, unconditionally and true, as if you had been working voodoo; I am stuck on you hard and can't seem to be able to break away, like something attached by welding, instead of just Krazy Glue. It is hard to think straight while you are gone, for wishing that you was here; whenever you aren't near, I have this certain fear, as if I might not get to see you again because you would disappear and then my life being close to instantly being over, as if I am driving toward a cliff and can't brake or steer. But when you are with me, I am in complete bliss; every single moment with every single touch sends chills down my spine, even when you give me just one single embrace with one single kiss. Every moment of passion places me into ecstasy; with you by my side, everyday is very nice, like paradise, to me. Like a devout Christian or devoted Muslim, I will continually pray and hope that the love that we share for each other won't ever go away; if I searched the whole world, I still feel that I won't find and be able to truly love another woman, as much as I love you, so why should I stray? I love what you are and I love what you ain't but we can't continue overlooking our flaws and mistakes and covering them up like an old, rugged house covered with fresh paint; we don't have to be as perfect as a glorified saint but must hold steady to each others' love and never faint. Any flaws that we may have let's burn down those bad habits and ways and then rebuild our hearts and minds with love and forgiveness, leaving out any hate; we can't wait to segregate hate and other negative emotions because they will deteriorate and destroy our houses of love once they fully begin to propagate. I will strive to continue to always be the best man that I can possibly be; some other men may fall short of stepping up and taking on full responsibility but I am not willing to ever be blamed for that type of delinquency. If I am going to love you and appreciate you, I am going to do it right; I will show you, both day and night, and not just after we get into bed and do intimate things with each other, after we cut off the lights. If I am going to show you love and respect, I will not only show you while we are alone and aren't around friends and family; I am not ashamed of you and my love for you so I will proudly display my love so that the whole world may see!

All Said And Done,
A Good Woman Like You,
I'll Never Find A Better One

A good woman like you is so hard to come by so that good woman in you, I never want to lose; between going from female to female to settling down with just one, in the past, it was so hard to choose. To neglecting to do right by you, as I should, I refuse; your full appreciation and gratitude, from me, is much past due. You have proven to me, over and over again, that you are much more precious and worthier than all the females that I ever had, yes, every single one; wait a minute to thank me for telling you something so nice and sweet because I'm far from done. It is me who really should be thanking you because you had came into my heart and showed me love at a point when I was feeling hopeless and all alone; when other females had tried to come get inside of my heart, I closed and locked the windows and doors to my heart and then pretended no one was at home. But you came along and showed me a type of love that I had never experienced before; after I had received a taste of it, I wanted so much more because you approached me with your true, pure love before attempting to give me sexual passion, as if that was all you have to offer me, so that I would see you as a potential companion for life, instead of just a cheap whore. Don't get me wrong, I am not into degrading females at all and calling them derogatory words other than their names; nevertheless, if I approached any of you females, acting and being anything less than a real and respectful man, more than likely, you all would do the same. I want to give you all of my heart and devotion because if anything ever came along to hinder you from being the wonderful and sweet female that you are now, I never want to be the one to blame; I also want to be the only one to give you my pure love, desire and quality time so that you won't ever have to try to get it from another, because failed love and relationships can become such a dirty game. Like a moth that is attracted to the light or a flame, I will always be attracted to your beauty, spiritual and emotional essence and intelligence without shame; for us to stay together, living in love, peace and unity, is my main aim. I don't want to hide my true emotions for you from you because I believe that they should be more evident; anything that I may have done to hurt you in any way, let me know so that I may apologize and then repent. I never want to live my life to the fullness, if that life with you I can not share; even if I lived over a century with great health, fame and prosperity, it won't be the same without you there because, for every part of you, your heart, mind and body, I will always care.

Things We Can And Can Not Do To Keep Our Love Strong

We can't lose what we have got because, with each other, we have a lot; any blemish or blot, mistakes and disagreements from the past that may have weakened our relationship, even the ones as small as a dot, I have already forgave and seem to have forgot. We can't lose what we have and can't lose what we had; now that we have endured many hard and trying times with each other, the good and the bad, happy or sad and joyful or mad, it all has made our love and passion for each other much stronger so now we must keep it all iron clad. We can't fuss and fight, all day and night; real men don't beat on women and put out her lights because a woman's inner and outer beauty, not bruised or scarred, is a much better sight. I love all women and, whether acquaintances, family, friends, lovers, in relationships with me, etc., I will respect and treat you all right; I would treat no race of women any better than the other, whether foreign, black or white. You can't ever cheat with another man and I can't cheat with another girl; no matter how beautiful and fine she may be, I can't afford to do it, whether she is blonde, brunette, red-headed, have long weave, has long braids or extensions, have her hair wrapped or have the pretty face with the baby doll curls. (Unless she is Beyonce` Knowles. Ha, ha, baby, just kidding.) We must stay with each other and we must pray with each other; we really need to be thankful to God and give Him the praise for His blessings and the strength to endure these hard times and we must give each other the necessary things to keep each other content so that we won't ever have to try to get it from the opposite sex of another. We must hold on to each other's love and never let go; we must never be ashamed of showing our love for each other in front of friends, family and others so that everyone will know. We must never ignore each other and neglect to give each other quality time; each special moment that we share will help ensure that I will continue being yours and you will continue being mine. We must listen to each other and never fail to communicate; if we wait and procrastinate, our problems may overburden us and cause even worse problems in our relationship and then it may end up being too late. We must make plans for our future and implement them, before we get too old; we can't be afraid to take risks, as long as they're logical, and step out on a limb to better ourselves, being solid, effective and bold. We must always look out for each other and pick each other up if we should ever fall; baby, I'll be there whenever you need me, all you have to do is call. We must sooner or later put a solid claim on each other, by settling down, after we marry; when others see a ring on our fingers, it will lessen being continually approached by every Tom, Dick and Harry or, with me, every Wanda, Sue and Sally.

Maybe We Can Live "Happily Ever After", After All

Sometimes, I wish that we could have that "happily ever after love" or, in other words, that "fairy tale love" but in this day and time that seems unrealistic; nevertheless, I wouldn't say that I don't believe in true love at all because being a cynical, unloving and uncaring person is just not one of my characteristics. If I am going to truly love you, I am going to give you my all, my one hundred percent; even if I don't get to tell you that I love you everyday, you will still know because it will be that self-evident. Live freely in my heart, because you are a co-owner and have to pay no rent; just repay me with the same love and passion that I give you so that it will always be a fair exchange and the payment won't ever be misspent. If you ever think that I would ever leave you for more beautiful, finer and sexier women, you don't have to worry about none of those; I could have dated and had a lot of them a long time ago but, to have a long lasting relationship with you, it was a decision I most gladly and certainly chose. A lot of women, like them, is so used to being catered to and cared for that they, themselves, don't know how to return the goodness or care; they may have been so used to being "given to" that they don't know how to "give back" or even share. I think that it should be fifty-fifty in the relationship so that it would be fair; I see too many people being manipulated and used by their mate, just to be mentally, emotionally and financially depleted or cheated on and I am not the one to go there. If it ever comes to this, the same way that you came into this relationship, is the same way that you can leave; I am not the one to help turn any female from sh.. into sugar just for her to leave and sweeten someone else's cake and Kool-Aid, you best believe! If we are going to work to try and have something better in life, we have to do it together; if I see that you are real in what you want to, or us to, achieve, I'm down for whatever and will ride or die with you in any type of harsh weather. I don't like to half-step or take one step forward and three, or more steps back; bad relationships, hard times, drama, disappointments, mental pain, agony and other life's struggles have beat me up and tried to keep me down all my life so now I don't give a damn about fighting back and also I simply refuse to mentally crack. Two is much better than one so, therefore, both of us working toward our goals and fighting through any of life's struggles, in this day and time, is much more easier than trying to do it all by ourselves; if you continue to show me that you are a real woman, I will prove to you that I am a real man and will work with and be with you for the rest of my life, until death. Just watch and see, baby, our life together will have a much brighter day; if we really try and truly believe, "happily ever after" may not be that unlikely, unreachable or seem so far away!

The Real Deal Of How I Feel

Baby, I love you from the bottom of my heart and my life being with you has really been a blessing; I always show and tell you how I feel with truth and sincerity, because I can't pretend and fake all this and I never took acting lessons. There is no other female in my life but you so there is no need to ever get rowdy and pull out a Smith-Wesson; I will try to never bring any pain, drama, disappointments, hate and broken trust into our relationship, so that you won't have to be like a priest listening to confessions (Doing wrong in relationships, in the past, and pulling through the drastic consequences have taught me a very valuable lesson!). And, no matter how upset I may get at you, you won't ever see me get violent; nevertheless, when things go wrong or we disagree, I will never hold my peace about how I feel and remain constantly silent. Honest and positive communication is one of the keys that we must have to maintain our devotion and trust; it is not something that we might have to do but is a must so that we won't ever have to tell our confidantes/ confidants of the opposite sex our business and later start having feelings for them and lust. If you are wondering if we really are destined to be together or have a bright future ahead of us, all I can tell you is most likely or probably; if you ever wonder if all of my emotions is real when I tell you all these wonderful things in poetry, they are, but although I may display my words passionately and eloquently, I really don't consider myself a prodigy. Everything that I say or write comes straight from my heart and is real; I will always show and tell you how I truly feel from now-until, you know the deal. All of my writings are authentic by me because there is no need to plagiarize them and steal; my feelings for you are so real but to whether or not yours are true, that's your prerogative and free-will. You don't always have to tell me that you love me because you show me more than enough; you always stayed by my side and proved to me that you still care, even when things had gotten rough. Now, I can tell you that my love for you is a lifetime guarantee, even if you never become my wife; I'd rather bring joy and excitement into the relationship from loving, respecting, appreciating, giving and spending quality time with you than getting a kick out of causing and keeping up drama, animosity and strife. I want our love and passion for each other to last a lifetime; I'll never hesitate to do what it takes to keep our relationship together strong, at the drop of a dime, so that we will continue to shine and you will continue to be mine. I always want your love and passion, because I don't think that I could get it any better from another; I will always love and care for you the same whether you are healthy, ill or fully healed and whether we are working together with each other financially or if I am the only one bringing home the bacon, the cheddar or the bread and butter.

Loving You For Life

Watching you, as you peacefully sleep, sometimes makes me want to joyfully weep; I would have no problem with waking up next to you for the rest of my life, because I truly believe that the love and passion for you I will always keep. My emotions run deep into my heart and soul, as you can feel them and behold; you mean so much to me and my love and passion for you will never go unseen and untold so that you can fully understand the true reason that I treat you as if you are much more valuable than platinum, diamonds and gold. You are the only woman just like you and no one else will ever be exactly the *same*. You treat me as if I was the first and only man that you ever had and, as far as women go, I hope that you will be my only so that's why I wish that I could show and tell you that I love you, as often as I say your name; no matter if my financial status change or if I gain fortune and fame, my love and passion for you will never go completely dry but be continually replenishing like the oceans after a heavy rain. Just like the oceans and sea, my love for you will never fully evaporate; I will never willingly give in to negativity and hate or procrastinate to show my pure, positive feelings because if you left me alone, or once we are dead and gone, our love and passion for each other would abate and then it would be too late. From my life until death, I will always try to give you what you need and desire and look at myself before I fault your wrongdoings because I want to be considerate of you and your feelings and not only think about myself; I will continue to stay with you, even if I gain

45

much wealth, because you have remained by my side to work with me, nurture my heart and mind from the sickness and pain of not truly being loved by other women and helping me regain my emotional health. Therefore, the healthy, refreshed love from my heart and the inspiration and initiative to work together to help better ourselves, from my clear mind, belongs also to you; my emotions for you runs deeply into my soul so that loving, caring, sharing, appreciating and, whatever else that you need from me, are things that now come so naturally and things that I never have to make myself do. You bring out better than the best in *me* and I will always strive to *be* all the man that I can *be*, even if I don't ever join the *Army*...Reserves; treating you wrongly and being any lesser would really take some nerve! You have given and catered so much to me so now lay back and let me serve; no matter how much I try, I can never be content and seem to be able to give you all I think that you truly deserve. Being your one and only man and doing right, day and night, is my main game plan; baby, you will always get my sincere love, sweet passion, deserving respect and appreciation, quality time, trust, caring, sharing and so much more, as often as I possibly can, because, no matter where life's journey takes us, you will always be my number one fan, understand?

No More Soap Operas and Drama, By Settling Down With Only One Potential Baby Mama

Baby, if you ever wondered if there are still some good men out there, as you can see, I am living proof; just continue to give me the chance, hold on to me and never let me go and you will continue to know the truth. Come and allow me to show you so that you can see how wonderful a true marriage, filled with devotion and honesty, can be; all the finer things you have always wanted in life and in a man, you will find better in me. I will treat you the right way, as a virtuous woman should be treated, because as a good man, I can not fail at that responsibility; I will make sure that our life together, with the love and passion for each other, be a whole lot more real, exciting and have less drama than all that soap opera mess you see on TV. If you ever start thinking that all that drama and *fighting* will keep our love life and relationship more interesting and *exciting*, you could keep trying to lure me into the mess but I'm sure not *biting*. With just one slip and I will see the hook but it will be a little too late; you would then have me in hot water and take me for all that I've got and leave nothing but my skin and bones on the plate. I have no time to fail and get in trouble over you to be in and out of jail; a lot of men claim to love their freedom but sometimes it's really hard to tell. Domestic violence and other associated and related violent crimes is on the rise and the prison population is constantly growing like flies; some women might get the men into the mess by instigating drama and telling lies, then when it all hit the fan and all hell breaks loose, causing him to do something that he may later despise, it will potentially land him in a jail cell while tears roll down her sad eyes. But I'm not going to say that it is always the woman's fault; some men just fail to give their women the proper love, care, appreciation, trust and respect, as they should have been taught. Maybe she'll sooner or later will take a beating when maybe she should have fought; then the woman might think that it is part of her fault and will allow him to keep doing the same thing over and over again to her until he is told on or caught. I could never do that to you, baby, and neither keep up drama and strife; how can I truly say and prove that I love you, if I beat you black and blue but later want to call you my beautiful, lovely wife and not knowing if, sometime in the future, whether or not you will try to get even by doing something like poisoning me or fatally injuring me with a knife? And I surely don't want to push you to, secretly or openly, messing around with different guys all over town, to later incline you to bring me on a talk show when you want to reveal the secrets to me, as the security hold me down so that I won't act a fool and clown; I don't want to be embarrassed and boiling hot, while you be laughing all in my face, and the only thing that I can do in return is look stupid and frown. I don't want to go on the "Maury Povich Show" as you reveal sexual partners or potential baby daddies whom I might or might not know; not knowing if I contracted a disease that will affect me quickly or kill me very slowly and being torn between forgiving you or storm off the stage saying stuff that I really don't mean, as I start cussing and calling you a nasty "whoe". Neither do I want to leave you and have a lot of other babies' mamas; I don't want to ever fully indulge in my past desires and fantasies of having many flavors of different women because, if I had my way, I would have kids in pajamas stretched from North America, South America, Africa, Asia, Europe, but especially in Hawaii,

Puerto Rico, Cuba and all over the Bahamas. Therefore, I don't want to picture myself going through all that because all I want is you; I don't want a lot of other women because I already had some of the good, the bad and the ugly so what else is new? If I gave some of you women all that I've got, you would still want more, that's why it's hard to give you all anything that you may ask for anymore; the economy is already shaky and if I took some of you women shopping, most of you would still pick up items for me to buy, nonchalantly, as easily as you would pick up beautiful shells that you may see and want from seashores. Gas and food prices are already on the rise and living life in general is already hard; therefore, I still don't understand why a lot of you women still don't consider this and continue to choose to max out credit cards? I am interested in discovering the cause of the problem that some of you women have, when it comes to spending, but I don't want to take the time to dig deeply into your psyche and get into the core; I can't afford to spoil any of you and refuse to allow any of you to have my pockets sore. Nevertheless, baby, I will give you as much as I can and what I think that you deserve, although sometimes you do get on my last nerves; all I ask is for you to appreciate it all and give me a lot more to look forward to from you, instead of only admiring and being turned on by your sexy bodily curves. I want to continue to love you from my heart and although I'm not perfect, trusting, respecting and appreciating you more is a start; the same way that I don't want to lose you, you shouldn't want to lose a good man that gives you a lot more than just a helping hand, if you are truly smart. So far, I thank you, sincerely, for being there for me and treating me so sweet and kind; in spite of all the drama that I see on television and the news, having a wonderful, caring and sharing woman like you help give me all that I wish to find: peace and harmony in my life and in a relationship and a much better peace of mind.

Giving Each Other Much More Than What Money Can Buy

How does it feel to have a man so real; to have a man that makes you feel much more than small change everyday but instead feel like stacks of hundred dollar bills? How does if feel to have a man that will remain by your side, regardless of if you are rich or poor, healthy or ill; if you want to see how superb your hand will be in this game of love, give me the cards and let me deal. Baby, I'm a pro in this game of love because it takes little skill; I don't always have to depend on how I currently feel but allow my love and other positive emotions flow freely from me, at my own free will. In this game of love, I want us both to win; I want you to be my lifelong partner so that you won't be manipulated and cheated out of your winnings in this game of life and love by some selfish and greedy men. My success will be your success, and vice-versa, and will be equally shared by the both of us; I will never take more out of our relationship than I put in, and hopefully it will be the same for you, so there will be no need to constantly disagree and fuss. "What's mine is yours and what's yours is mine" don't always work out, most of the time; especially, when there becomes a point where you are contributing dollars worth of assets into our relationship and I am only contributing nothing but pennies, nickels and dimes. Sometimes, you may end up with more money than me or, at some point, I may have more money than you because it just ends up that way; as long as the one that has less pull their weight in the relationship and contribute in other ways that money can not buy, the other partner should have little or nothing to say. If you ever have less, I have no problem at all with helping you out; having it all with none of you will never keep me happy, no doubt. But if you ever reached a point where you love the money and material things more than me, I'd have no choice but to cut you loose and set you free; they may say that "love is blind" but before I let you or any other female ruin me, emotionally and financially, I will damn sure make myself be able to see. Hopefully, as long as you continue to love me for me and never let money change you, we will never be faced with that danger; it's funny how sometimes, when people have less, they stay by your side but as soon as they get a little money in their pockets, and until they are about broke again, they sometimes, more so than not, become distant strangers. All these truths, you should already know from experience, even before I had written them or before I spoke; even if I had plenty of money and everything I want in this world, without your love, care, respect, appreciation, with you giving me the joy and other things that money can't buy, my life would be as dull as a bad joke and I would just be better off broke!

Having Natural Attraction To Other Females Don't Mean That I Will Go Get Sexual Satisfaction

Baby, I am only returning the love, respect and appreciation that you have given me so there is no need to feel that you need to reimburse me; I will always try to water our relationship with truth and honesty to help relieve you from the drought of searching for true love and the desert and desolation of past lies, infidelity and broken dreams from others, just in case you are still feeling thirsty. By maybe being hurt and disappointed in the past, I know that sometimes it's hard to show me your true emotions and show me how much that you love me to the fullness but you must trust me and give me a chance, if you want our relationship to last; I don't want to rush you into moving too fast, but after you take some time to stop being afraid and come out of your shell, don't hesitate to talk to me and be free to just be yourself, if that is not too much to ask. We will never be perfect, no matter how hard we may try, in this life; it is not even guaranteed that we will remain faithful and true to each other, if we become husband and wife. That don't mean that we shouldn't put forth a strong effort to keep our relationship together and stay devoted; we should be eager and proud to move to a higher level and position in our relationship, like someone whom had been working so hard doing small, menial tasks, for a long time, on their job but finally has been promoted. We will eventually make some mistakes in our relationship, as you will, sooner or later, be seeing; try not to get too upset if you happen to witness my natural attraction to other females because that is my manly nature that you won't ever be able to stop from being. Nevertheless, I won't disrespect you by intentionally staring, approaching other females or sneak and do it when you are not around because I don't want you to do it to me; I can't neglect to have restraint and keep myself in check, when I have any desire to let any other woman fulfill any of my sexual fantasies. I will come only to you when sexual passion and satisfaction I want to receive; why go to another woman to get passion and sexual satisfaction that I may want and need when one of the main goals of sex is just a climax that I want to achieve? No matter how good another female's sex may seem, in the end, the climax will hardly be any different from the one that I can get from you; therefore, it makes little sense to me to go out and mess around all over town so that is something that you may never have to acknowledge that I do. Only because another female may look and could perform better, it might would make the climax more intense and feel a lot better, especially if she is tighter and wetter; nevertheless, I never would want to mess things up and go there though, because one night of pleasure will give me a longer time of hurt and pain once we lose all of what we had, things that she might never be able to fulfill or satisfy me with, when you leave me, conspicuously, or after you write me a "Dear John" letter. Since only you are mine, I will give just you a hundred percent of my quality time; even for the moments that you are away, every second you will still be in my heart and every minute you will be on my mind. No other woman will ever be able to replace you, no matter what sweet words that she may say to me or no matter the enticing things that she may do; if you ever doubt that it is true, remember, each day and night, I am coming back to only you.

Why Try To Beautify What Is
Already Pleasing To My Eyes?

Closer and closer is what I want our love, for each other, to always be; come closer and look into my eyes so that your beautiful and smiling face I can see. Don't worry about what society's concept of beauty is because, as some people say, "Beauty is only skin deep"; the beauty inside of you magnifies your outside beauty so never allow anyone to implant a different opinion in your head so that you start believing it and start selling yourself cheap. Some people that is considered nice looking, with a snobby persona, may be pleasing to the eyes for many others to see; nevertheless, when I witness them looking down on others, acting like their sh.. don't stink, that really irks me so much that they really begin to start looking ugly as hell to me. Everyone will see you differently, baby, and be *opinionated* but they are not the ones in whom you are *obligated*. No matter what you try to do to please others, they will never, hardly, be completely satiated; therefore, if you want to be continually changing who you really are and how you actually look just to please others, as long as you are with me, I can't let you, I hate it! If you want to make yourself up, sometimes, to please yourself, I guess that is fine; I am the one who will be looking at the real you when you come home to pull off that mask, anyway, ninety-nine percent of the time. So, it is me in whom you should really be aiming to please; I am not talking about the times we are alone and you give me much more than a simple strip tease.

Make-up is just a simple cover-up; if you put make-up on, before you leave home, people will never see the real face that you have in the morning, that I see, when you wake up. You will never see me changing the way I am, for a disguised person for others to see; I am proud of who I am and there is no person in the world that I'd rather be, but me, and if others can't accept that then they can go on about their business and let me be. As long as I take care of my own self and don't do anything to personally hurt or offend others, I will do and say what I want, whenever I want, at my free will; I don't give a damn what others think about me because I am not their responsibility and I take care of myself and pay my own bills. Therefore, I will walk how I want to walk, talk how I want to talk and say what I want to say, anytime and anywhere, night or day; I refuse to change myself to try to accommodate others' way of thinking how I should be because I, myself, and God above, are the only people, since I am grown and out on my own, that I really have to answer to each day, even after the hair on my head turns gray. Love who you really are, on the inside, instead of focusing primarily on the out; whenever you start doing that and then pretend that you don't have self-esteem issues, I start having doubt. Whenever you have unexpected company over, you rush to make yourself up and make yourself what you call, "presentable", almost about to break your neck; I guess you would commit suicide then, if you ever suffer irreparable damage to your face from an accident, like a car wreck. I love who YOU are, no matter how others think of you and how you *look*. All the fun moments that I spend with you is so special that I want to enjoy them over and over again, like a good movie or book; even when old age comes to rob you of your youth, like a crook, I will still be there to affirm to you that you are still beautiful and protect your self-esteem, like the king is protected by the pawns, knights, bishops, queen and rooks. Love who you are and I'll love you the same; I will always be proud of who I'm with and will love to say your name. I will always love to caress your hair, face and body, without shame; for you to see yourself, as lovely and beautifully as I see you, is my aim.

Enduring Through The Present And Past To Help Make Our Love Last

I need my passion to rush upon you like a flood as you become baptized in my true love, to make us as close or closer than relatives by blood; I want my true love and desire to explode and consume you fully, because others didn't quite do the job since their nonchalant attitude, uncertainty and restraint made their intentions of love a complete dud. I never would want to ever get so angry at you that I hunt you down and be a menace, like Elmer Fudd; whenever we get upset at each other, we should come together, be civilized and compromise so that our tears of joy will wash away any anger and frustration, like being cleansed with hot water and cleanser suds. I must get over my fears of messing up in the relationship, a phobia and curse that has plagued me for years; I can't allow anger, pride, jealousy, dishonesty, distrust, misusing trust, having lust for other women, etc. to bring you to tears and cloud my judgment with indiscretion, to be like someone that has drunk too much liquor and one-too-many beers. We have to stick together, for our own good, no matter what our family, friends and others have to say; if we want to be strong in each others' love and go on tomorrow, we have to make any and all wrongs right today. I want to love and be there for you, night and *day*. No other makes me feel the way that you make me feel, because its so true and real, therefore, why should I stray; when things seem to not go right as they should, I must continue to love and hold on to you anyway to keep the remaining love and passion for you, inside of my heart, from fading away. I can't imagine life without you by my *side*. Together, we are a formidable team and force, like Bonnie and Clyde; if I don't get to make it up to heaven with you whenever I die, I just have to be miserable without you in hell, as I arrive inside to bust it open wide. I might not always seem like the perfect man but I'll always be the best man that I possibly can; being with you long term, to build a successful life with you, will get much easier over time, if you just would take the time to consider things and understand. The hard times and pains of today won't always be there *tomorrow* and nothing but happiness and joy can come after the *sorrow*. We have to be strong and resilient to deal with the pressure and cruelty of this world, that's becoming so much of a horror; I wish that I could go back in time to share the good times our ancestors shared in the past, if only for a short while, because those happy times I wish that I could borrow. Without love for ourselves, each other and other people around us, we will never get back *there*. It feels so much better to me, not to hold and keep all my blessings and love to myself, but to share; we must not only reserve our blessings and unconditional love for each other, family and friends but whenever anyone in this world is feeling hurt, disappointed, down and out, I really wish that I could show them all that I really, truly care!

Us Loving Each Other, More And More, Is What I Really Hope For

I know that previously in the past, I might have done some things that would not make me seem as your ideal mate; nevertheless, I realize that now I have to come real and clean my slate. I intend to become and mean so much more to you than just being someone that you used to date, to becoming someone that you will truly come to love and appreciate. I know of no female that is more deserving of my love and passion than you because, with all that we've been through, you have always remained by my side and stayed true; with all the love that you have shown me, I have no choice but to give some love back to you, too. What else can I do but be true and real to a female that seems as if it is her life's mission to love and care for someone like me; we may be different in a lot of ways but it is a lot that attracts me to your individuality, you see? I love the way that you look and the person that you truly are; you may not be famous in other people's eyes but you will always be my superstar. You are a star that shines brighter, to me, than the Sun, moon and other stars *combined*. I have no problem with giving you a lot of my time; you will always stay close to my heart, for others to see, because there is no shame in my game with calling you mine. We have to protect our love for each other at all costs; if we continue to invest all this time and energy into each other, just to later grow apart and let it all go to waste then we'll both be at a loss, true or false? I want to fully solidify our relationship and take it to a whole different level; I will be consistent in treating you right, both day and night, instead of one day treating you with love and care, as if I am a child of God, and the next day raising hell, like I am the son of the devil. Loving and respecting your heart, mind and body, as if they are my own, is a must; how can we say that we truly love each other, if we don't have any trust? We must stay focused on loving and pleasing each other, in every way, so that for other people we won't start having lust; we have to communicate constructively because we get less accomplished when all we do is argue and fuss. I will never simply blame or accuse you of doing wrong, without proof, and be in the danger of leaving; if you show me enough times that the love just isn't there anymore and that you no longer care, I'll probably leave then because then I'll have a better reason. You have shown me, continually, that you are the only female that I should settle down with and marry; I will, hopefully, be able to stay by your side until the day that I die so that I can be a father, instead of just a baby daddy, to any future children of mine that you may carry. As good as you are to me, treating you any differently would be like a crime; as long as you continue to love, respect, appreciate and stay devoted and faithful to me, as you are now, my love and passion for you will last a lifetime.

Thank You For Giving Our Newly Marriage Life A Life Worth Living

Despite all the drama and hard times that I've been through, in my life, I'm so glad that today is a day that I can truly smile; both the better and worse days that we've shared together was all worth the while because we're ending our relationship as just partners and beginning a new life in style, as soon as we finish walking down that aisle. I cherish every single moment with you and the good times that we spend together, I never want them to end no time *soon*. I love the closeness of us being together, the fun and exciting things that we do and what we share that is not based solely on sexual intimacy and later destined for doom; I really am determined to show and prove to you that I still love you, honestly, as we hold hands under both the Sun and stars and is not in all that big of a rush to get you to myself, privately, in a room for our honeymoon. The old life of sowing my wild oats, as a bachelor, is over with and through; I'm giving that part of my life up for you, the very moment that I say, "I do!" It would have been just a wild fling and other things, if I wanted our relationship to end in brevity; I'm not looking to go from being a spring chicken to an old fart all alone in an empty home because, as the years have gone by, I have grown to yearn and desire some type of longevity. I am so glad that when we were contemplating and making plans for marriage we were both on the same page; instead of worrying about an uncertain future and other problems that we may have to face in life, now we have being with and there for each other to look forward to as we continue our journey together toward old age. I know that the road won't be easy for us, as it haven't been easy for others that have been down the same road before; if we ever begin to constantly argue and disagree, without compromising, I'll keep walking out the door until things cool off and we can communicate sensibly, before I allow our issues to build up to a point where we just can't take it anymore. We both will have our differences and different ways; nevertheless, we have to learn to positively communicate, compromise and live together in respect and peace so that the years that we anticipate being with each other don't turn into only weeks or days. I continue to hear constantly about married couples separating and getting divorces and having many complications and drama once the proceedings of court litigations finish running their courses; therefore, I believe that we should communicate constructively and put a very strong effort to work out our problems ourselves first, if we can help it, before we start letting other people into our business and trying to get help and advice from too many different sources. I want to go back to the days when marriage really meant something special, other than an incentive for some business dealings and tax returns; I might not know all that I need to know about our marriage deal but I am certainly most eager and willing to learn. The old habits and ways of the single life, that we had before, those bridges and connections we have to get over and burn; it might not be easy at first but over the years, through experience and maturity, we'll be able to make a perfect one hundred and eighty degree turn. Everyone will have their faults, no matter how simple or complicated, but to run from you and any problems that we may have in the future, I can't easily be abated in manhood or persuaded; once we fully pull through, from the efforts of both me and you, and start living life day by day in love, peace and harmony, it will be more serene, alluring and relaxing than the most beautiful music being orchestrated. Each and every time that I look into your *eyes*, I never want to fail to *realize* that as long as we stay true, love, appreciate and respect each other, sincerely, without giving it to infidelity, deceit, jealousy and *lies*, the time that we spend together never *flies* and, most importantly, the love and passion that we have for each other will flourish and never *die*. Each and every day of the year, I can't wait to see the results of how successful and wonderful our marriage life will be; as the years go by, it will be very wonderful and beautiful to see as we create our own legacy and begin to form our own branches on the family tree.

The Power Of Our Love

For every flower, there are many bees; for every bird, there are a lot of trees. For every blade of grass, there are many drops of dew; nevertheless, for all of me, there should always only be one of you. It seems that I was made just for you and you were made for me; together, we seem to make things run more smoothly, you see? When we walk and hold hands, the sun seems to shine brighter; when we hug and kiss at night, the stars and the moon seem to gleam whiter. When we talk and cuddle with each other, from trees, the leaves seem to tumble; when we make strong, passionate love to one another, lightning seems to flash and thunder seems to rumble. When we run and play with each other, the wind seems to blow and when are crying, joyfully or sadly, rivers seem to flow; when we are distant from each other for a long time, it seems to snow. Don't you see the power of our love; it is represented by an olive leaf in the mouth of a dove. Whenever we are together, nature seems to be in order and at peace; if we ever broke up with each other and grow apart, I hope and pray that the world won't cease!

The Value Of Our Love

I could buy us a new house and I could buy us a new car; I could travel with you to places, domestically or afar. I could buy you expensive jewelry, accessories and clothes and take you places few other people may go; what would I be trying to prove and what would I be trying to show, though? Doing all this, without having your true love means nothing to me; by buying and doing all this, I still may not be the type of person that you really want me to be. I want to be the one to love you in sickness and health; I want you to still love me through indigence or wealth. Even with lots of money, if I am not the respectful, appreciative, loving, caring and compatible man that you want me to *be*, things won't be better than if I treated you right and kept you happy with me while having less, you *see*? I might not have the money to always buy you nice things and take you on exotic vacations; I might not even have the time or the financial expense covered to be able to travel the nation. As long as I have you, I have much more than wealth; being without you wouldn't be good for my mental and emotional health. Having you and your true love is something in which I can always rely; I couldn't purchase anything to make you love me, if it is not truly in your heart, so I wouldn't even try. The joy of having just enough in life with a lot of you sometimes make me want to just break down and cry; my loving, respecting, appreciating and adoring your heart, mind and body, sincerely, to keep you happy with me so that I can see the beautiful smile on your face each day, are certainly things money could never buy!

Irreplaceable Love

I could lose money and I could lose possession of a house or car; I could lose all the fame that I could attain here and afar. I could lose time and I could break and lose a rare and expensive bottle of wine; I could lose valuable treasure that I may never again find. By losing these things, I could get over it or eventually replace; anyway, having much more than you need is very stressful and takes up too much space. Your beautiful eyes, sexy lips and lovely face, I could never replace; stay as close to me as you like because you don't crowd my space. I'll never find another you because you are one-in-a million or one-in-a billion; you are even one-in-nine hundred and ninety-nine trillion. Your tantalizing body with every single *touch* are just a small part of the reasons that I love you so *much*. Your loving and caring heart, intelligent mind with the heart-warming smile on your lovely *face*, these things, and so much more about you, I could never *replace*!

The Versatility Of My Love

My love for you can be sweeter than honey and much more valuable than money; it can satisfy your soul and fulfill the hunger and desire of your needs and passion like a good meal fills your tummy. It can reach higher than the sky and be deeper than the deep, blue sea; it can be the light that reveals how wonderful a real relationship could be so that your blind eyes may be healed and finally see. It can be the clothing, coat, scarf, gloves and boots to help protect you from the coldness of the hearts of others that might would want to cause you physical or emotional harm; it can be the shelter and heat to keep you warm and help protect you from some things that may rush upon your life suddenly and unexpectedly like a storm. It can be more precious than the most valuable jewels and brighter than the closest star; it can be like a child that misses you and loves you the same, whether you are near or afar. It can get inside your heart, soul, mind and body to help heal pain from bad experiences that maybe you have had from life's experiences, if you just give it time; it never will be selfish because I want to share it with you, instead of only giving it to others or just claiming it as only mine. As long as you stay by my side and remain *true*, that is how long I will always love you.

Problems

Love Is Strong As Steel And Yet As Delicate As Glass

Love can hurt, if you abuse it, be untrue and put no effort in trying to make it work; even the most loyal dog may turn on you, if you abuse it, dog it out and treat it like dirt. Love can be as fragile as glass and grow much quicker than grass; if you get in the wrong and aren't careful with it though, it might become like electricity mixed with water to knock you dead on your ass. But why would you misuse or abuse something that can be so *pure?* You should think things over or just let it go, if the love isn't real or if you are unsure; just try to be considerate of the other person's emotions, before you allow them to love you and then you leave and let them go, or else you may leave them with an emotional ailment for a long time without a cure. Why would you try to hurt someone, when you have feelings too; why would you want someone to stay faithful and real to you, if you yourself is promiscuous and untrue? What, are you doing someone how someone else did *you?* It is not the right way to handle things and try to *do.* Do you try to get back at a store, when you think that they charge you way too much; do you try to get back at some friends and family members, when they continually ask for favors but hardly ever or never stay in touch? Do you try to get back at the government, when they take out all that tax and seem to waste a lot of your hard-earned money from your *paycheck?* Would you try to get even with a former job in which you gets laid off or fired, after you have worked so long and hard on so much that it that it seemed as if you was about to break your back or neck; would you try to get even with the alcohol industry if you, a family member or friend, gets so drunk that any of you get a D.U.I. or get into a car wreck? Would you try to get back at the tobacco industry, if it causes you to have health problems, like emphysema or lung cancer; would you try to try to bring hurt, disappointment and pain to the things and people you lose money to, as in bills, gambling or blowing money on lottery or an exotic dancer?... Hell, no, most of you won't or don't: I already know the answer! Some things just happen or they are things of bad judgment, with consequences, that we sometimes bring on ourselves; only because we believe that one, or more, person, place or thing caused us emotional, physical or financial pain/harm, it don't make it right if we take it out on someone else. If you don't try to do right or treat others how you want to be treated, after so long, any good that you may have done in your life will ultimately be defeated; whenever, later on, you try to do right and instead things go wrong, you will then feel really cheated. Whatever wrong you do to others will, one way or another, come back on you, sooner or later; therefore, you shouldn't try to bring a relationship with your spouse, loved ones and friends down but help it continue to rise, like an inclining escalator. When you love, instead of having animosity and hate, somehow things in your life will work out for the good; if you don't consider the fact that when you hurt others you can be hurt yourself, you really should!

Sometimes, Even A Player Gets Tired Of Playing

There comes a certain point in a man's life when he gets tired of playing females, like cards, and fooling *around* and tries to find that special one to settle *down*. I know that you are that type of woman that I can love and enjoy for the rest of my life; a woman that I can build a better life and relationship with and one day cherish as my lovely wife. At one point in life, I was afraid that any true relationship I would ever have wouldn't last; in the past, I was so used to drinking, chiefing, partying and chasing after a lot of ass. But you are that strong woman that helped bring about a change in me; your love, care, trust, desire for only me, patience, etc., helped uncover the veil over my eyes to make me realize that the bad habits that I had, and you despised, was just a ongoing cycle that would keep bringing me down so now I can finally see. As long as I have you, I never want any of those things to ever be part of my life again; I have to be very careful though and focus on resisting temptation and loving, pleasing and desiring only you, since I am still living in sin. I have to continually pray for God's help, ask for forgiveness and thank Him for His blessings, especially you, every day and night; I can't afford to start slacking and neglecting to love, care for, respect, appreciate and treat you right. But it takes two, so please just try to continue to do all the right things that you know to do; if you be good to me, baby, I'll damn sure be very good to you! I will strive to do all the right things, before you can even ask; I have to take the initiative and take on responsibility, like a man, if I want our relationship to last, because no strong and lasting relationship is an easy task. It is never fun and games like how the children play, such as "ring around the rosies, a pocket full of posies", or won't always be like a bed of roses; if we aren't careful though, it will instead be hidden, empty condom wrappers, strange, lost boxers and drawers concealed everywhere with unidentified negligees, thongs, panties and panty hoses. And I don't have time to be beat up or cut up; I never want us fussing, fighting and busting each other in the mouth, just so we will shut the hell up. I'd rather be single and alone, before I go through all that; sometimes, I already look too unattractive for bruises and my lips are already, kind of, naturally fat. Therefore, let's save the drama for the soap operas, talk shows, news, estranged boyfriends and girlfriends, husbands and wives and baby's daddies and mamas and all the fighting to the dogs and cats, boxers, martial artists, soldiers and fighting cocks; as long as we do what we are supposed to do and stay faithful and true, our love and bond to each other will always be on lock and solid as a rock. To whether we stay together or break up, to later maybe be trying to make up, is a choice that belongs to only you and me; we are the only ones to possess each other's love and passion in each other's hearts, to be able to open it up and give and receive more, so please don't lose the damn key!

Sorry For Taking So Long To Help Make Our Love Strong

I know that sometimes it seems and feels like you are unappreciated and I talk to you as if you are uneducated; it seems that, whenever we disagree and argue, things can't even be negotiated because we bring our family's and friends' input in with our problems so that our minds become too saturated with negative feedback and adulterated. We shouldn't even be affiliated with jealous haters that can't wait to see us separated; they may not come out and say it, bluntly, but they sure as hell insinuate it. Therefore, we should start being congregated with couples that has been together for years and didn't have to "fake it to make it"; if we endure our relationship for a decade we would then be congratulated and, into the "club of ten year or more anniversaries", we would be proudly matriculated and incorporated. Free from the guilt of our relationship becoming dissipated, we would definitely be exonerated; sometimes, our love and passion for each other won't flow freely but, every once in a while, have to be mentally and physically stimulated so that in time they will become more concrete and perpetuated. I never want to reach a point where our relationship gets so old and dull that later we start making love only because we feel that we're obligated; I never want to start telling you, when you want some loving, "That's okay, I already masturbated!" I, simply, want to get fully inside of your heart, to help keep us from allowing anything to tear us apart; I want the latter times of our relationship to be as wonderful and fervent as the start. Let us work on each others' imperfections and improve our strengths, until we are molded into each others' heart and minds, as precious pieces of art; we would then be more intertwined, your love and passion mixed with mine, until it would surely hurt to ever part. If I ever left you alone, it would be so wrong because you continually keep me joyful, is spontaneous and never play out like an old song; you excite me, fully, whether I am embracing you throughout the day or either at night when you strip down to your thongs and have nothing else on. For now on, I will keep trying harder to be persistent at treating you right and keeping you happy with me, making it a habit; every time that I get a good opportunity to spend good quality time with you, surprise you with an occasional gift and hold and tell you that I really love you with a kiss, I am going to reach out and grab it. Because, every missed opportunity to do the right thing is an opportunity of lost time that I will never be able to get again; you want the fullness of my heart, mind and body as a prize so, hopefully, one day soon you will most certainly win.

Why Be Against Me And Fight, When All I Want To Do Is Make Things Right?

At first our relationship was wonderful and as fine as can be; you believe that things are still the same but I tend to disagree. I have given you plenty of love, without you returning as much to me; you have driven my heart, with my love and passion for you, out to the desert and the tank is about on "E". I can never allow you to bring me down though and destroy my chi; being in a relationship that both of us could be happy in is more of my cup of tea. I try to uncover the veil over your face so that your blind eyes can actually *see* that you may never be able to find a man that puts up with you like *me*. You don't know how to appreciate and respect a man that treats you right because maybe you are too accustomed to being treated *wrong*. You don't know how to look beautiful in a dress, since some other men was only wanting to see you in tight pants, shorts, short skirts or in a thong; you don't know how to accept a man that wants to communicate positively, when most men you've dated wouldn't, most of the time, admit when they were wrong or even pick up the phone. You don't know how to keep a man by your side, when most of the men you've had wouldn't even stay at home; now you sometimes gets ill-mannered whenever I want to spend some good quality time with you so maybe you should be left alone. If you can't satisfy me mentally, it will be harder to satisfy you emotionally; if you can't satisfy me emotionally then I will feel less of a need in helping satisfy you financially, sexually or devotionally. Here I am trying to give my all before you even have to ask me, personally, or call; at a time when you used to ask other men for support, it seemed as if you were talking to a brick wall but now you expect me to support and come to your aid quickly, whenever you need it, and not procrastinate or stall. If we can't pull together, there is no sense in being together at *all* because, as I said over and over again, together we will stand and divided we, definitely, will *fall*. And it seems that every time that you do things that threatens our relationship and is contrary to my best interests, it seems as if I am a U.S. soldier and you are an Iraqi soldier or a *man* in Al-Qaeda or the *Taliban* in *Afghanistan*, fighting and hating on me, mostly because I am an *American*. I'd rather be your lover and not a fighter; I want to stay honest and true, not be a scandalous backbiter. Our relationship is much bleaker and darker but I want it to get back brighter and whiter; if you don't want our relationship to burn to a crisp then put down the damn gas can and lighter. If you cause it to burn, you might as well just let it go because it will be too far out of control; if you keep treating our relationship like crap, I will not keep tolerating the stench and will dump and flush it right down the commode. Lastly, I will bury it deeply into the ground; it won't make any sense, after that point, for you to try to communicate with me or even come around. But if you really want to save the relationship, better start cleaning up your act and hurry up and grab the Bleach, ammonia, Lysol, alcohol, hydrogen peroxide and, maybe, even Listerine; it will be too late once it starts to rot, gets too filthy and disgusting and lose its feeling, after it gets gangrene!

Don't Hurt And Kill The Relationship, When The Pain Of It All Is Something We Both Can Feel

I really want things to work out but, actually, I don't see the use; the pain of it all is hurting, poisoning and slowly deteriorating my heart, mind and body, like the effects of consecutive bites of many black widows and brown recluses. And once it spreads, without proper aide, our relationship will be dead; you will be torturing and killing me, slowly, without the evidence of bloodshed. There will only be my heart and mind lost in a void; if other females try to come get close to my heart, I will get all shaky and paranoid. After that point, if a relationship that I may have is based on only sex, with no strings attached, then it might would be cool; if I nurture and take care of a bitch and she turn around and bite me once she's at fault but, if I allow her or another one to bite me a second time or more, then I am the damn fool. Again, I don't get into degrading females at all and calling them derogatory words other than their names but if I treated any of you women and acted any differently than a real and respectful man, more than likely, you all would do the same. I know that many of us men have been like dogs and have bitten and mangled women so now some are starting to bite and fight back; I can only do the best that I can to treat you the right way that you should be treated but if another dog have harmed you in the past, hell, I can't change that. What I can change and rectify is any wrong that may come from me; now, if I promise not to harm and bite you, will you try not to play and hurt me?...We'll see! I have learned long ago not to bite because I know how much it can hurt; playing with someone's emotions can be disastrous so, with that danger, I won't flirt. Why play with fire when it can burn; if some people want to play, let them play because, no matter how much or hard it harm and comes back on them, some people never seem to learn. Love is a lot less stressful than animosity and hate; some people find out a little too late, after they had a great mate but denigrate and depreciate the relationship, until it starts to deteriorate, and now they are back to integrate on the single scene having to date. Why invest all that time and energy into the relationship, just to later let it all go to waste; if we can't get over small, petty problems without arguing and being on the verge of breaking up, why be together in the first place? Love is about giving more than you take, being true to your mate and never fake; it's about not only be trying to stay together for the kid/kids' sake and loving each other, equally, regardless of how much the other makes. Love is giving, even if it your last and doing special things for your partner before they even have to ask; I know that it won't be always be an easy task to keep this relationship from ending sooner than we expected and way too fast. Let's try to work out our differences, hold on and act like we know from right and *wrong*. I'm tired of all the disagreeing and arguing because I'd rather be civilized and get along; if we can't do that then sorry, baby, I'm gone!

Killing My Past So That My New Life With My New Woman Will Last

As the days go by, I contemplate on past memories of the past relationships, with all the infidelity, disrespect and lies, and was once mesmerized by all the visions of the past, so much that I want to break down and cry. I'm too much of a man to allow tears to fall from my *eyes* but I'm nevertheless *surprised* of how much it hurts when old feelings, with the bad memories, come back up from the past that I try to bury in the back of my mind and *hide*. All the false alibis with *lies*, selling females broken dreams, creeping and flat out cheating, not spending enough quality time with the females that was mine, being unappreciative, disrespectful and not showing enough love, but only doing things that females *despised*, has made me more considerate and *wise*, as I think back and remember all the final *goodbyes*. What was I trying to accomplish and what was I trying to *achieve* by doing all those things and much more, in the past, that now I can hardly *believe?* I should have given more than I received and spent more time with the children that I previously helped conceive; I should have been more honest about my feelings with my women, instead of trying to play on their emotions to manipulate, deceive and later leave. I should have followed through with plans of being some female's one-and-only man; two is better than one so it would have been a whole lot easier trying to have something better in life, with the right female hand-in-hand. Now after all this time of feeling wrong and all alone, I can finally understand that it takes a real man to keep a real woman and make a house into a happy home; you never miss the oasis of a virtuous woman's love and devotion until it is all dried up, they pack up and is gone. Now, the pain of past playing, manipulating, lying, dead beating and cheating, disrespecting without giving enough affection, wrongful demotion without devotion, etc., is coming back to haunt me once again; I used to laugh inside at being called a player, believing it was a game in which I could actually win. Now, I realize that, like a seed with the outside shell, that old part of me has to die so that the new man inside of me can bud and bring forth a new life; no more multiple female partners but now I am finally looking forward to settling down and having a lovely wife. Bad history can repeat itself, if we don't learn from it and make a positive change; I hope that any new lady never hesitates to let me know if I start to change from the way that I should be and start acting despondent and strange. My life would be her life and her life would be mine; I hope and pray that my past life continues to stay dead and living a life, as a new man, becomes much easier over time.

Let's Take Some Time To Show Each Other That I Am Yours And You Are Mine

Have we told each other, "I love you", today? I think *not*. Have we told each other how much we care and appreciate each other? We, obviously, *forgot*. I know that we had been working a lot and have been so busy, causing a lot of stress to be on our chest; although we have been through a lot but is currently more blessed, we must still continue to show and tell each other how much we care, regardless. If we don't take time to show each other affection, maybe someone else *will*. It don't take much time and don't require much skill; just brief moments of affection each day that's real will help keep us from distancing ourselves from each other and acting with ill-will and will keep our love fervent and strong, you know the deal. The only way that affection will not be effective is if you don't want me no more; I wouldn't allow you or any other woman to remain with me just for convenience so therefore, if your feelings are not there anymore, I'm not going to stop you from leaving out the door. Sometimes, we can't only show love but would like to hear it too; sometimes, when we have doubt, we need further confirmation that it's real and true. Since we don't get the same type of love and affection elsewhere and don't get the same respect and appreciation that we show each other, I don't want to bring any burdens, stress, ungratefulness, disrespect, hate, animosity and other negativity that I might had experienced in the day and take out on you; baby, you know that this is a dog-eat-dog world and sometimes is wilder than the wilderness so why should I bring back to you the same type of pressure and stress that I have experienced throughout the day and have been through? When we are off work and is not busy, we should make some time in the night or day to be romantic, flirt with each other and play; we have loved each other too long for us to allow things to start going wrong and cause us to start going astray. I hope for the day that our love will be firmly planted, unwavering and will always stay; we should take some time to solidify the relationship and each other into the better person that we want each other to be, knead, mold, fire and glaze it all into a beautiful piece, like finished sculptured clay. I used to hope and pray constantly each day to have a beautiful, fine, intelligent and independent woman like Beyonce'; nevertheless, having someone that beautiful and fine that didn't love and care for me like you do, I would trade her for the type of true love and passion that only you can give me, anyway. I know that we have been busy lately but we should still take a little time out for each other, if only ten or fifteen minutes; every minute of every hour that I spend without you feels like nostalgia and loneliness but every second that I spend with you feels so ecstatic and splendid. We are working too long and too hard for a man/woman that don't understand that all this work and no play in our relationship is beating down our relationship harder and quicker than a beating that would come from Bruce Lee, Jet Li, Steven Segal and Jackie Chan; our relationship might be slipping through our fingers, slowly but surely, quicker than two open hands full of sand. Therefore, we have to find a way to compromise and spend more quality time with each other, the best way that we can; our brief, quick hugs, kisses and goodbyes in the morning, with no time in between, is just not working so we should come up with a much better plan.

I'll Never Try To Rectify
A Lie With An Alibi

I am sitting here, all alone, wondering how things went from being so right to being so wrong; the day before everything was fine and dandy and the next day, you're gone. I had later found out that you had left because of a small truth told to you surrounded by a much bigger lie; what I'd like to know is why should I even try to rectify any lie with an any type of alibi? Later, by me, the truth was *told* and although the issue was *old*, it caused a lot of drama and damage, once things had started to *unfold*. Although I was scrupling before revealing my situation to you, I, myself, never lied; nevertheless, if I had told you about the past circumstances from the start, maybe, I would have saved you the time, energy and disappointment that caused the confusion to make you leave, break down and cry. Even after I had clarified and justified all the mess caused by all the lies, the damage, nevertheless, was still done; instead of waking up easily from your touch and kiss upon my face in the mornings, now I wake, reluctantly, from the rays beaming in my eyes from the light of the sun. You had told me that maybe you would come back, once you had thought things over and relieved all the pressure and stress from your head; in the meantime, as I am trying to be patient and wait it all out, I am much more stressed out myself, more than I have ever been in my life, and is in an emotional and mental void, as if I am brain dead. It's hard to display any excitement and happiness because, without you by my side, I'm sad; I can't express the relief and joy of elucidating my past situation with you, because the fabrications told to you by the other party has made me too steaming mad. Despite all that was said and done, it is best not to act, vindictively, but to just get over it and forgive; being stressed out, infuriated and administering retribution for the lies with other scandalous lies or however else, isn't the right way to live. What goes around comes around; once it's all and over with, I will have the last laugh when I go on with my life and see it excel and the scandalous ones come out looking more stupid than a clown. Then we maybe could rebuild our life together and keep people out of our business; as time goes by, you will see that I would never do anything to hurt you in any way, intentionally, and both you and God above will be a witness. So, the jealous haters can hate and I don't really give a damn who else participates; to being reprehensible and always keeping up drama, I am too mature and strong-minded for all that to ever stoop down to their ignorant level and be able to relate. Only because they don't have much of a life or much going for themselves, deep down inside, they envy and want to try to bring our joyful and successful life together down; this I guarantee you though, if we stay together, in time, we will steady climb the ladder and continue to see their life being miserable and them crawling around on the ground, looking lost and wanting to be found. I will keep working to build us an even better life than now and give over a hundred percent of my best; I have to keep on being grateful to God and let Him handle the rest. Finally, once all this is over with and done, I will try to never allow any problem like this, or worse, come into our lives and bring our relationship down again; we'll let the childish-minded adults play their silly games because I know who in the end will win, my friend.

I Wish That I Could Go Back
And Change The Past So
That Our Love Will Last

From the time that you had left, I only have experienced pain and misery; before you had left, the love, peace and happiness felt better than paradise in my heart but, ever since you went away, it feels like all hell broke loose inside of me. I just close my eyes sometimes and wish that all our problems would simply go away and disappear; nevertheless, once I open my eyes and reality slaps me in the face, I'm surprised to see, it seems like, a hundred times more, compounded with the stress and drama, staring at me dead in my face and into my eyes right here. Misery just loves company but I am just not the one to complain; if I don't talk to anybody though and keep all this locked up and building up in my brain, my sanity and complacency, I might not be able to maintain. If I can't express myself and talk to *you*, who else could I trust or turn *to*? If you could hurt and turn your back on me, after all that we've been through, I don't even want to imagine what this cruel world could do; if things was really going that bad between us, I wish that you would have at least left me a clue before just up and leaving out of the blue. I wish that I could only go back and make all our wrongs right so that I could continue to be able to hold you tight, throughout the day and into the night; I wish that we could have spent more quality time with one another and romancing one another with all the hot, bubble baths, wining and dining and dinner by candlelight. To have things back to where they used to be, I would go to any and every extreme; I figured that things would become "peaches and cream" again, once we had compromised and you had blown off a little steam, but I guess that was just a broken dream. I see that I was wrong, after acknowledging that you are still gone and I am still broken-hearted and all alone; if I continue to have too much pride to give you a sincere apology, so that you may condone, and you are too stubborn to take an initiative to make a conciliatory call over the phone then our little spat will just go on and on. Why must all this *be*? It beats me; what you actually don't see is that is that if we reconcile and come back together, in unity, we can both live together freely, happily and as successfully as a long, lasting legacy. Hopefully, then I can regain my sanity and hold on to my full dignity, without suffering with any more despair and humility; you may think that I have gone about crazy for wallowing in my temporary insanity and misery but, hell, you was the one who did it to me! I know that you have to be feeling some type of hurt and pain, since you went away; the way that we continually loved each other, night and day, the way that we teased each other, before intimate foreplay and all the other wonderful, quality times that we spent with each other was so special to us and so real that I believed that it would have been more of an incentive to want to stay. I suppose that the negativity started to outweigh the positive and our relationship wasn't strong enough to last, without resiliency; I wish that I had more things to be able to hold on to you, sentimentally. But I don't and it feels so wrong; everything that we had for each other seems to be all gone and I can't continue being hurt and feeling sorry for myself, from dusk until dawn, so…sorry, baby, so long!

Our Love For Each Other Is Now Gone So Now I Must Get Over It And Move On

Our houses of love for each other have crashed down and I'm still trying to clear away the rubble; I, initially, tried to ignore the obvious signs of trouble and now, because of procrastinating, I tried to work twice as hard to patch things up on the double but you deliberately burst that bubble. I'm not trying to put all the blame on you because I have my faults, too; on the other hand, most of my feelings and actions toward you have been loving and true so tell me what else can I do? I am not going to just "fake it until we make it" because there is no fake in me; I don't have to work too hard to be the man that I'm supposed to be because, ever since I had begun to take on more responsibility in life, manhood came naturally. And I have no intention at all to stop being a real man now; even if I don't get to continue fulfilling my life of being your man, I am still going to continue to be a good man, anyhow. Before, you were a very important part of my life; even through the animosity and strife, the love and devotion that we had for each other overcame it all to cause me to reach a point of wanting you to become my wife. That's why I don't put my trust in feelings, because of their fragility and tendency to change; therefore, I base what I feel for you on faith, because I know, before I can actually see it happening, that we could always love each other and keep that love and passion strong and in close range. But now it seems hopeless for us and I am seriously considering not even trying to save our relationship anymore; why should I continue to allow you to beat my heart down to the ground, stomp on it and leave it painfully hurt and sore? The more I try to hold on to you is the more that you seem to back away; I could easily get another woman any day so there isn't no way that I am going to ever beg you to stay. On the other hand, if you wanted to try to overcome our differences and compromise to regain the love and trust that we had, I'll give my all, my hundred-percent; I am not going to allow myself to give a thousand dollars worth of my love, though, compared to your fifty-cents because, at this point, my love and desire for you is almost already gone and spent. You have to deposit some real love and passion into my bank of love, if you want to withdraw some out; I'm not going to give you any more interest-free loans and if you don't pay your part of the mortgage of true love and devotion, for me to allow you to live in my heart and mind, I have no choice but to foreclose and put you out, without a doubt. Only because I very rarely argue and shout, you may think that I am playing with you about what I am talking about; you just keep thinking what you are thinking then and you will soon enough see, firsthand, as I show you better than I can tell you that I am not playing and my words will become crucial actions and have much clout. But if you want to do right then I'll act right; before it is too late, you better come out of the ignorance and darkness of not realizing that it will be hard to find a better man than me, which puts up with you like I do, and start to see the light before I am long gone out of sight! Then you may never, ever find the same love that I have for you now, ever again; it will be as if I will be living in the serenity, joy and righteousness of a new, blessed relationship while you will, most likely, be lost, alone and living in promiscuity and sin.

I Don't Think That You Will Truly Be Happy With Anyone Else

I can't imagine you being truly content with another man, now that we are separated, because you two just won't fit; even if he has a lot of cash, is handsome and physically fit, that really don't mean sh.. It makes no sense to start all over again with someone else because we have invested so much time and energy into each other, although the current situation currently makes us uneasy and tense; there is no way that you can get me to believe that another man will love and care for you more than me, because it won't be easy to have me convinced. Even if he can buy you more than I could, would you consider that real love; if he was better looking and makes better love than I do, is that really the type of man that you always had dreamed of? If you were feeling down and out, would he be there to put up with all your stress relievers and listen to all the problems and drama that you want to talk about; if you become ill or hurt, would he be prepared and come to your aide, like a good boy scout? Would he have what it takes to make a relationship last, without having much cash; when problems and hardships come crashing down on the relationship, would he stick by you to help pull you through or get ghost and dash? Would, both he and you be able to get along with each others' family and in-laws; would he be the dull, unappealing but educated type or the wanna-be-cool type that wear baggy clothes and bust slack in his pants, showing dirty drawers and have a little too many flaws? Would he appreciate a good woman and show you the proper love, appreciation and respect; would he be the type that takes all his problems and negative emotions out on you, to beat up on you until he almost breaks your neck? Would he be able to get along with you long term and not fuss and fight, throughout the day and night; do you believe that, even if you aren't and don't be all the woman that he had expected you to be, would he still continue to love you anyway and treat you right? Would you be prepared to wake up to that same face every morning, if you ever became his wife; if you asked him for help doing some chores around the house, do you believe that he will help out or just sit there scratching his head and looking dumb-founded, like the "Andy Griffith Show's", Barney Fife? Would he stay with you to take on full responsibility, if you have kids together, or would he leave you all alone so that you would come crawling back to *me*? No, you wouldn't because I would have gone on about my life, happily, and would let you suffer the consequences for your own mistakes and of leaving me and will just let you *be*. You may think that I am asking too many questions but these are questions that you should be asking yourself; I just don't want to see you with anyone that you will be miserable with, later on down the line, and mess up your life so much that you would almost welcome death. As long as you remain with me, I will stick with you through both thick and thin and sickness and health; I will always be the one to care about you and be concerned enough to help fulfill all your needs and desires, to help give you physical, mental, emotional and sexual wealth.

Helping Me To Change For The Better Changes The Mood Of Our Relationship To Nicer Weather

It takes a real woman to make a real man; it took a lot to change my stubborn ways, but to the other minor flaws that you can't quite help me get rid of, thanks for doing the best that you can. After being together for a while, aren't you surprised of how I just metamorphosed right in front of your eyes; it feels much better being a loving, devoted, faithful, respectful and appreciative butterfly than being a lowly, stubborn, promiscuous, unappreciative, disrespectful and scheming caterpillar so full of lies and alibis. Even now when I attempt to pull a fast one on you, smoothly, you calmly reply, "Nice try!"; when I try to get your aide, support or approval of something that you don't quite think is right, you simply ask me, "Why?" When I don't tell you the full truth, you impatiently tell me, "Don't lie!"; I realize that I have to completely change my ways so that your final words won't ever be, "Goodbye!" Sometimes, when you don't fully trust me when I am trying to do the right thing, I argue and get mad and later feel bad because I disappointed you and made you sad; I want to let you know that I love you and I apologize, from the bottom of my heart, because I realize that you just want me to be a better man so thank you, sincerely, for being the best woman that I ever had! I know that I have to be more considerate of you and your feelings and put them first because, before I had found you, bad karma and relationships was coming back on me harshly, like an unbroken cycle, and was also like an never-ending curse; between juggling around with different women that I didn't truly love and all the past playing, lying, scheming and everything else coming back on me and haunting me, I really don't know which things was worse. With all the pressure and stress of too much responsibility that I just wasn't used to, relationships became tense and *terse*. I felt like any day my head would burst and things was so bad in my life that I almost welcomed the hearse; I felt that way, until you had came along to give me a better outlook and feedback on my life and relationships, to help me implement a positive change and also gave me so much more that it would be very hard to repay you and fully reimburse. Now, I have no problem at all with being the best man that I can possibly be; I appreciate and acknowledge you trying to help me to better myself so that it no longer offends me because I now understand, truly. Since I am becoming more of being on your level and state of mind to see things eye-to-eye and do things hand-in-hand, I want us to save more money, settle down and buy our own house with our own land; what I am actually trying to insinuate and say is that you becoming my wife, as I become your husband, is my ultimate plan. I love, appreciate, respect, want to give you more than I receive and want to spend much more quality time with you and that is not about to change; I hope to never become anywhere close to being the irresponsible, stubborn, unappreciative, disrespecting, lying and scheming man that I used to be or either become worse, by becoming mentally deranged and acting despondent and strange. I promise to put forth my best effort to never stray and go back to my old ways; as long as we continue to compromise, pick each other up when we fall, never be judgmental but understanding and remain strong in each others' love, our relationship and life will see much better days!

Our Love And Passion Growing From Saplings Into Trees

I want us to hold on to our love, if there is just a seedling of love there; I would cherish that love and nurse it back to full health to let it know that I haven't abandoned it because, baby, I still care. We both have to maintain and care for that love for each other, nurture it and constantly keep a warm atmosphere for that love to grow; it will surely perish, if I maintain a healthy, rainy season for it in my heart but you either keep a dry, drought of displaying love and passion back to me or keep cold and bitterness in your heart so much that it continually snow. If we left each other and started all over again, to put our love in the heart of *another*, the love between us would choke and inevitably die, as if we gave it absolutely nothing to drink but continually fed and stuffed it with a whole lot of bread and nutty peanut *butter*. The type of nourishment that we water and put into it determines the health of the fruit of the relationship that grows; if we put hate, jealousy, infidelity, disrespect, neglect, etc., more into the relationship than love, then the love and passion for each other will never flourish so don't pretend that you're naïve and don't know! Love and hate will never be able to live with each other, in our hearts, in the same house; we can't continue to have both of these feelings for each other, in our hearts and minds, so one of them really have to get the hell out. And if we decide to put hate out then we have to put out all of its friends; if we clean up our relationship with the love, joy, peace, care, devotion, faithfulness, passion, etc., I'd be damned if I allow the jealousy, infidelity, distrust, disrespect, neglect, etc., to bring hate back in just to dirty and mess things all back up again! Love and hate will always be rivals; since the hate has almost deadened and exacerbated our tree of love, to cause it not to have the strength and vitality that it used to have, I think that our love life and passion for each other needs a big revival. Our love is still joyful in my heart and I want that love to continue to abide; I want to stay true only to the love and passion that I have for you so please try not to do anything at all that would make me absolutely turn away from you and backslide. Whenever you want to know something simple about me, as simple as how I'm doing, some of your eagerly gossiping family and friends never hesitate to over exaggerate and fabricate things about me when they give you a daily or weekly update; the lies and half-truths seem to just go and on and never seem to abate. Any of our family's, friends' or any other's negative input on our relationship only will choke out the roots and rob the nourishment that we give to our love and its fruits, just like weed; when people try to give us their negative input about us, we should put our hand up in their face and eradicate the thoughts, like Weed-Away, so that their input won't get into our mind frame and begin to feed because what we feed our mind sometimes also nourishes our heart, therefore, that negativity is something we most definitely don't need. If we put forth a resolute effort, we will be able to see how beautiful and strong our relationship will really be; I will be so proud when our love grows long and strong, from just being like a sapling to being like a Sequoia oak tree!

Although My Heart Still Aches, You Were Never A Mistake

If I ever thought about telling you that I don't love you anymore, I would have already lied; if you are waiting to see tears roll down my eyes, from the pain of us going our separate ways, you won't because I have already cried. Crying and showing painful emotions from all this is something that you won't ever see me do; I am trying to be strong enough to pull myself back together so I want you to do the same thing, too. I know that it will be a lot of misty eyes after the final goodbyes; if we did move on to someone else, instead of working things out between us, learning from everything that we have gone through will hopefully make us a lot more stronger, considerate and wise. Both the deliberate and unintentional disappointment and pain that we have caused each other must have been much more pressure, added with the outside problems, than we could take; nevertheless, I will never regret being a part of your life at all because it was never a mistake. If I hurt you in any type of way, I apologize sincerely, from the bottom of my heart; I still love and miss you so much that it will be a while before a new relationship with someone else I begin to start. The end of the road between us is a road much too short; I don't want to talk about and reflect on the circumstances that brought us to this point in our lives, because a cynical response I don't want to retort. Things are already shaky enough between us so I don't want to make them any worse; I will shake off any inhibition that would cause us not to at least be friends because I am considerate of the feelings that you still have for me and want to put those feelings first. I can't lie and say that the feelings that I had for you are entirely gone; now, I must swallow those remaining feelings and store them in the back of my mind so that I won't feel so hurt and disappointed when I think of you whenever I am all alone. During the time that we were together, things felt so right but now it feels so wrong; instead of feeling romantically inclined and joyful, after hearing love lyrics on the radio and reminiscing on the good moments that we shared together in the past, now I get the blues whenever I hear those songs. And the blues always seems like bad news; although the words in the songs were written about someone else, in our past life together, a lot of those same words most definitely become as true as if they were talking directly to me and you. Then I start feeling so disappointed and very deserted; nevertheless, I will never stalk you, just to try to get back next to you so that I could later try to fulfill past sexual fantasies that I had for you, like an obsessive person that's also sexually perverted. While we were together, whenever you came around, I could always run to embrace and kiss you gladly; now, whenever I see you, I walk away like a dog with its tail tucked between its legs and head low to the ground, very sadly. I can't continue to go on, pretending and crocodile-smiling like everything is alright, because I do that very badly; although I am upset, I don't want to be or remain on bad terms with you and have any animosity and other hard feelings in my heart, because I never like to end any relationship madly.

I Won't Settle For Less But Will Try To Be At My Best

I refuse to believe that having a successful relationship and marriage, in this day and time, is unrealistic; I acknowledge that many relationships and marriages have failed in the history of mankind, but I don't want to become a statistic. Why should I waste time, though, with a female that shows early signs that she won't always be mine; I, myself, am too defiant and wary of relationships that just won't work to try to hold on to it anyway and waste time arguing, whining and crying. If it hurts too much to stay and you two can't work things out, it is sometimes easier to simply walk away; at times, if the love is strong and you want to still hold on, the pain seems greater trying to break away but after it's over with and done, it always later become a much brighter day. But if the love is true, I'll try to hold on because sometimes you never realize how much value and preciousness you have in a woman until she is all fed up with things and is gone; it seems so wrong to let thing get so bad in a relationship that the two have to talk only on the phone from different time zones, while one is freezing their butt off all alone in a blizzard and the other had gotten over the relationship with a new partner, laying back and enjoying ice cream cones. Some women work so hard to try to turn a dog, player, thug or scrub, etc. into a "Mister Right" man; if he won't come to the God above, that made him, to help him change his life and ways then how in the hell do you think that you can? And some men try to hold on to a no-good, gold digging, scandalous, backbiting, etc., woman or girl; other men already know that she isn't worth a dime but he gets seduced and tricked into trying to give her the world. She maybe already doesn't have nothing or much in life, besides what he or someone else gives her, prefers to keep up drama and strife and don't really want to work with him to have something better in life; is this the type of woman that he believe that he can or even would want to turn into a housewife? You can't help change some people, male or female, until they are ready to change their own self; if they don't come to grips that they are wrong, they will carry the same old bad habits and ways until death. Different people that have those characteristics think that they are alright and okay or even born to be that way; you know, they are just like some people who proclaim and are happy that they are gay. I will not be fooled into falling in love with a woman that is just not right for me and later be looking crazy, like a clown with an upside-down *frown*. I have learned that trying to be with someone that is not willing to help build you up will only keep your life down and it will be very difficult to get off of the ground; I refuse to play the fool for any female's amusement to constantly be disappointed and tricked, like how Lucy does Charlie Brown. I have also learned to treat any female with the same love, care and respect that I would want a mother, grandmother, sister, aunt or cousin to be treated; if I ever neglected to take responsibility and be the good man that I'm supposed to be then my purpose in trying to do right in life will sooner or later be defeated. But I won't settle with trying to do right by and sticking with a female that don't give as much into the relationship, to always only feel despair and cheated; why try to hold on to something that just isn't right for you because you certainly can do better and really don't need it. And you good females, be careful of any man that treats you like a doormat instead of a queen, acts too chauvinistic, sells you too many broken dreams and wants to be the only one in the relationship to be treated imperial; if you allow him to dog your heart, mind and body out, have too many kids by you then leave you, then afterwards to anyone else, neither one of you will really be marriage material. So women should always make getting an adequate education, career, a substantial sum of money in the bank and their own life together a priority before trying to find a man; in that way, if you get one that don't want to act right, you can be the one to tell him to get the hell on and still be able to maintain, instead of him leaving you and then you start struggling to try to make it the best way that you can. I can't understand that with some men that actually believe that dominating and walking all over females is the right way to be a man; it is a much wonderful sight to not have a female walk behind a man with her head held down but stay by a man, side-by-side with her head up, proudly walking hand-in-hand. If you both work together in the relationship to help bring and keep the relationship together, you will eventually have more than you need, like an overflowing cup; it might not always be monetary gain that you obtain but you will have love, peace, happiness and so much more in the relationship and those valuable things can never be spent up. I will also never understand some men that pretend to be happy with a female and go with the flow; nevertheless, they have sexual activities with other men, secretly, on the down low. Some of them might think that giving their female companion a little oral stimulation, down below, is so nasty but meet with other men in parks and other secret places after dark, just to give them or receive, a blow; what they don't realize or pretend not to know is that by them having unprotected sex with men and later going back to their females for sex, it is helping to infect America with more AIDS cases and killing it slowly, many years in a row. Those same men, some of them have double standards because even if their female be with another man or experiment sex with another female, they would curse them and the relationship and maybe even want to beat her and call her a cheater; what's good for a man to do to their female in the relationship is also good for a woman to do back to him so if he can't handle that, it's best that he leave her. Both women and men should wait until they're financially, mentally and emotionally able before trying to produce a newborn boy or girl; having unwanted or improperly cared for children is just not right because they never asked to come and be born into this cold and heartless world. So they should always be loved and have the best life has to offer, until they are old and mature enough to make it out on their own; if you try to raise them right and then they grow up, past eighteen years old, thinking that they have life all figured out, don't want to listen to good advice, be disrespectful and don't want to do something useful with their life, then let them go and try to make it on their own because they're grown. In essence of all I'm saying, everyone, please just love, care for and treat your mates with the same love, appreciation, attention and respect of how you would want to be treated; it is already too many hardships, drama, gloom, hurt and pain going on in this world today to bring more into a relationship, or even to other people in general, so we should all spread much love, peace and joy because, in this day and time, we all really do need it. Showing love toward our loved ones and others is something we should never hesitate to do; those of you who treat others wrongly, just like pissing into a strong wind, it will always come back on you.

Although Our Feelings Are Quelled, I Still Wish You Well

I am sick and tired of breaking up in relationships but I try not to let it show; every effort that I try to put toward making things right and better sometimes seem to go straight out the window. Is it that I'm just reaping what I *sow*? I really don't know; I mostly try to do right so that I can get good in return but I can never be absolutely perfect though. I remember the times when we really enjoyed the moments of our love and passion for each other that always seemed to easily flow; we always stayed true and faithful to each other, never cheated and kept things concealed and secret, on the down low. Now that the life and luster has left from the relationship, my countenance no longer have that peaceful glow; I hardly want to even look at you now, let alone touch, although in the past, I relished seeing your face, and at times, massaging and washing you from your head down to every single toe. I am now torn between remaining single or finding someone new; I don't want to listen to and hear from my family, friends and other acquaintances, sooner or later, about the next chance of marriage that I somehow blew. I don't want to be stuck in the house, in the mist of summer or winter, feeling miserable and despondent and telling my friends when they want to go out somewhere that I am sick with some type of cold or flu; I don't want to be so absent-minded and out of my head, thinking of how I lost you, that I have to constantly turn back around and return home from going to work or any other important business dealings simply because I left something that I really need, such as a shoe. I try not to ruminate and worry about us being apart, but what else can I do; I thought that I had the chance of being with the seemingly perfect person for me, in my life long term, and those opportunities are few. I remember us fussing sometimes at night about each other hogging too much space on the bed; I am more miserable now and still toss and turn because, although I can stretch out anyway that I want, I have just empty space to hold onto instead. If I see you out with someone new, sometimes my temper boils and my face seems to turns red; I try not to get upset or allow jealousy to come into my heart because I don't want to go to prison for life and mentally suffer, being without any female companionship at all, only because I accidentally hurt someone critically, or worse, by doing something much more severe than just knocking them upside their head. I don't want to be at home wondering if my children are being taken good care of or being properly clothed and fed; I hate it when I start getting angry wondering if you are allowing another man to get close to and tuck my beautiful children in bed, while you tell me a whole different story about how things supposedly are and I be misled. Don't let me hear of anything bad happen to my children or that they are being severely mistreated or unfed because I really don't want any crazy thoughts going through my head that you and whatever partner that you have would then be better off dead; thereafter, I most definitely don't want to stay antsy, agitated and on the edge hearing on the news about how I murdered someone, how out of the country I fled and is trying to elude authorities because I don't want to be turned over to the Feds. Nevertheless, I don't want to keep seeing you with someone new and, by seeing that it bothers and upset me, you rub it in my face and gloat; I then find someone that looks and haves herself together, more so than you, so that we may both have jealousy and discontent in our hearts and be in the same boat. I don't want to have to put on a charade and appear happy and content but, in actuality, be resentful and contentious of you for being alone and about the new issues, drama, problems and other burdens that I would then have to tote; you then watching and observing my life and misery, as a specimen under a microscope, laughing and telling your friends and folk, hoping that I end up on dope or already wrote a suicide note. You could try to bring me down all that you want but I firmly would say nope; there are many other logical and sane ways to deal with this and much better ways to cope. I don't plan on going to prison for life, worrying about being in the shower and trying to not drop the soap; I am not going to be celibate and devote myself to a higher purpose in life, without a wife, like the pope. I'm not going to live life in misery and I'm not going to mope; as long as I am healthy, alive and wise, there is always hope. Nevertheless, on the other hand, I'm not going to wish evil upon you so I really wish you well; it seems that in the past that I was hooked on your love spell but, in time, it seemed as if the potency has finally failed. The things that we both owned together, you can either keep, give away or sell; I don't know if my material, emotional or mental loss is greater: it's kind of hard to tell. I can't only fault you alone for your wrongs because both of our crap smells; that's why I can not fully justify telling you to get out of my life and go straight to hell. Whether we will do better once we are completely apart, only time will tell; we should look at other people that has been in our shoes before and, hopefully, it will ring a bell. I assume now I have to go back into the sea of life to fish for me another female so, into the beautiful and peaceful sunset, I'm about to sail; don't work too hard, baby girl, at trying to find another, better me because I don't want you to strain yourself or break more than just a nail.

Passion

Taking Some Time Out To Play After A Long Day

We have gotten out of the shower and is still soaking wet; if you want to continue our love making session in the bedroom again after we finish our shower then, baby, it's a bet. We have worked so long and hard all day so now it's time to play; isn't doing a little something-something to relieve all the tension and stress off your chest was something you wanted to do anyway? You don't have to be a freak. Just be my freak; let us freak each other for a long time, until we get completely weak. I'm not trying to turn you out because I just want to turn you on; as long as I satisfy you as much as I want you to satisfy me, is that so wrong? I like how you kiss and suck my neck and chest and slowly work your way down below: you know what I'm talking about; I'm talking about how you have fun working that mouth and tongue until I...ooh, baby, let me shut my mouth! I love your kisses, embraces and caresses, every single touch; the little things that you do for me, added with the bigger ones, are just a few reasons why I really love you so much. This is our private little game in which we both could win; this time you be the master and I'll be the genie so let's play again and again.

Working On You Is Like Working On A Second Job

Baby, now that we are both home from work and have a little free time, let's get showered and out of these clothes; afterwards, we can go back into the bedroom and do some private stuff that only we and God knows. There is almost no limit to the freaky things that I will do for you; if I work long hours and hard on a job for a man/woman that I barely even know, I know damn well that I can put in at least an hour or more, overtime, of foreplay and making sweet love to you. Then later I can hold you very tightly throughout the night; I will surely sleep more peacefully tonight, knowing that I treat and do you right. As I treat you as a queen and you treat me as a king, nothing can inhibit us as we do our thing; with our love and passion strong, nothing can hold us back in the bedroom, as we let our freedom ring. I have a dream that we will be together, seemingly forever, with most days being peaches and cream; we can't become monotonous and we must stay spontaneous and compromise so that the hard times in our relationship won't be as bad as they seem. It will be a lot easier if we do it in unity as a team; we are not just going to shine for others to see but we are going to beam. All my time today, with you, is what I want to proudly devote; put the phones on vibrate and off the hook, lock the doors and don't even think about touching that remote!

Feed Me Until I'm Full

My heart's and body's blood/sugar level is getting low so I know it's time to feed; your love and passionate food is all I need. So let us feed each other that love/passionate food until we are both full and can't eat any more; did I fill your plate more than you did mine or did you give me more...wait, why are we comparing and competing for? You can eat all you want now and it will still be plenty to eat later; you can start from the top of my body and work your way slowly down below and then back up again, like a busy elevator and suck on me like you would suck on a lollipop, Laffy Taffy, Tootsie Roll or Now-and-Later. Whenever you are ready for me to eat that good love/passionate food, ring-a-ling, ring-a-ling, make the triangle chime and I'll sure enough be coming to get mine; whenever you have the passionate food ready, fresh and hot, with you looking so sexy and smelling so exotic, you are never too hard to find. We can devour each other's passion on the bed, in the shower, against the wall or on the floor, as long as we don't forget to lock the door; come eat all you want until you get full and can't eat anymore. Don't be embarrassed or ashamed, baby, fill up your plate; if anyone else come along to offer their love/passionate food, we should always tell them that we are full and already ate. I love to snack on the "neck bones" of your neck, the "rump roast" of your butt and the "cantaloupes" of your breasts; everything on you tastes so delicious that I have no favorites or best. I love the chocolate covered cherry of your belly and the good, hot and juicy piece of fleshy crevice and meat between those thighs makes me melt quickly when it gets hot, like butter or jelly. But we shouldn't just feed each other only passion, like only meat in the diet, but also the vegetables and fruits of pure love; we shouldn't just feed each other passionate sex, because sex alone won't keep our relationship alive, but also feed each other all the love, care, respect, appreciation, quality time, with all the other big and small things that we do for each other or dream of. Walking together holding hands, embracing or cuddling each other and making future plans is some of the type of love food that I want to give you also so please understand; I love you and never want to indulge and devour the love/passionate food of another because I am proud to have you as my only woman and I am proud to be your only man. We should never allow our love/passionate food to spoil or grow old; I'm so glad that all of it digest smoothly into our heart's, mind's and body's stomachs so that we never need anything like Tums, Ex-lax, or Pepto Bismo. So come feed and you can surely be greedy; I have more love/passionate food than you will ever need so I have no problem at all with feeding the needy.

Our Fiery Sex Drive Helps Keep Our Relationship Alive

Girl, for all the love that you always give, I have much appreciation; the heat of passion between us is always hot and flammable, like the gas in the pumps at the gas stations. Don't be afraid of the rush, baby, give your sex drive plenty of gas; as long as it is just me and you pleasing each other fully, there is no danger of moving too fast. Let's not drive too fast, though, because I want our love-making sessions to last; I want to always satisfy you to the fullness as I continually tap that…Ask and let me know what you desire and need because I am always willing; we will both have a ecstatic, exotic feeling as we give each other good "sexual healing". I want to continually give you pleasure because I know that we are both tired of constantly feeling disappointments and pain; I won't just give you my love and passion but I am going to let it rain. Like a *shower* that pours every night and day and every second of every *hour*, you must let it consume your heart, mind and body, like fire, to satisfy you to the fullness because, as long as you allow it, I have that *power*. And the love and passion that you give me, I am so ready to devour; I will show you much love, respect and appreciation for it all so that the love and passion that we have for each other won't ever spoil and go sour. I want to get plenty of it, while the getting is good; your love and passion is the best, better than the rest, in this neighborhood; oops, let me shut my mouth and knock on wood! Do I give you as much love as you give me? I *should*. Will I try to give you anything that your heart desires? Well, I *could*. I might not always will be able to give you what you want but I'll give you all of what you need; if you are ready to receive the best of my love, give me your hand and I'll take the lead. I'll be loving you more than you need during the day and giving you even more loving after dark; I want to explore the different parts of your body that few or no men have ever been before, as if I'm Lewis and Clark. I want to explore the flatlands of your neck and the mountains of your breasts; your body is like a candy land in which I want to lick from east to west. Sometimes, I don't even have a problem with licking you from north to south; just make sure all of your body is squeaky clean though before I start putting stuff into my mouth. Finally, when I begin to explore with my submarine into your deep, wet sea, your body will get much pleasure coming from me; I want to get you very hot as I hit the right spot to raise your body's temperature to a higher degree. After it's all over and done, I hope that we both is satisfied enough to have a peaceful sleep; sometimes, it is so good that I want to joyfully weep and I can dose off, quickly, without tossing and turning and counting sheep like Little Bo Peep.

Our Love And Passion Must Stay Strong, All Year Long

From January to September, you give me sweet memories, from past occasions and events, in which I love to remember; from October to December, I love cuddling close to you, to stay warm from the cold weather, while you become limber under the sheets and as you keep my manly nature hard like timber. Whether it's warm or hot, I will always display my love and passion for you a lot; any issue that we had been or may be arguing about, I already forgot. I don't want anything to inhibit us as we make sweet *love*. My body upon and inside of your body, with certain body parts fitting snug and tightly as a glove; I like it all, baby, whether I am on top or you are on top working your stuff from above. You have no problem with giving it to me and allowing me to give it to you, just the way I like *it*. You seem to read my mind to fulfill my desires without me asking, as if you are psychic; no matter how much I try to hold back my true feelings and full passion, I always explode with more and more so I decided to stop trying to fight it. I can't take it when you give me your non-stop loving and I can't fake it when I cry out in pleasure when you do all the freaky things that you do, just the way that only you create it; I like the way you shake it when you tease me and please me and I really love you so much that I know that we can make it. You don't only satisfy me with sex but you also make me content with all the love that you have to give; you give me as much, or more, love, care, respect and appreciation as I give you so, hopefully, the rest of the days of my life with you, I want to live. I'm glad that sex is not the only thing that keeps us together; as time goes by, things could change for the worse but I hope it never. All the hugs, kisses and caressing, with every single touch, are just some of the reasons that I love you so much; I also cherish you for all the quality time that we share, being there for me no matter what, us picking each other up when we fall, helping each other to succeed, fulfilling each other's needs and desires and such and such. The way that you kiss and lick me from my neck, down to my manhood, sends chills down my spine; baby, I'm so glad that you are mine because everyday you make me feel so divine. Your good loving keeps my head spinning as if I had been drinking strong wine and afterwards laid back and sedated as if I had been smoking potent weed; nevertheless, at the full heat of passion, you keep my heart pumped and exercised like I had been doing aerobics and racing with full speed. Me sucking on your neck, sucking and licking your breasts, licking and kissing the navel on your belly; afterwards, I like stimulating and entering the sweet spot between your legs that is wet, sticky and sweet as jelly. I have no desire to do the things that I do to you on no other female, have no fear; baby, your loving is so good that I have to have it day after day, week after week, month after month and year after year.

Getting You So Hot That You Don't Want Me To Stop

Baby, we have been together for so long and, to me, you are still so sexy and fine; I love to look and admire how beautiful you are face to face but I also like to see and desire, from time to time, your body from behind. You look so wonderful when you're dressed but even more tantalizing out of your clothes and after you slip the shoes off your toes; later, when we start to make love, I'll take my time to satisfy you, fully, because you are my lady that I want to please completely, instead of me just wanting to get off, as if I was with two dollar whoes. I'll always treat you right because, to me, you are more valuable than both platinum and gold; you look so good that I know that you will still turn me on enough to make me want to make love to you, even when I am sixty or seventy years old. When I make love to you, I always have to do it properly; if another guy tries to hug, kiss, rub or love on you, in an intimate way, then let him know that he is at risk of being shot for trespassing on private property. I know that I have to tell all those other females the same; you let me know that we belong only to each other when we make love and we only call and scream each other's name. Allow me to take you to ecstasy and bliss and please don't try to fight it; I'm going to get your body hotter than a bottle-rocket firecracker, after I completely ignite it. I know that my job is almost done once you start bucking like a wild horse and we rock the bed harder than the possessed girl did on the *Exorcist*;

me, caressing, kissing and holding you tightly is the primer for the explosion of your orgasmic bomb but the sucking, licking and sticking will be the catalyst. I will start detonating it by starting to lick and suck on your neck and then lick and nibble a little on your ear; before the time that I finished working the foreplay any lower on your body, if you were a Spanish female, I wouldn't stop until you tell me, "Papi, yo kiddo coger!" I would then start to rub and lick on your *breasts*. I know that when I make love to you it feels good but try not to bang your head so hard on the headrest; if your breasts was any bigger, baby, I would need a compass to find my way around as I lick them from east to west. Even if they were just a handful, I would lick and rub them just the same; as fine as Little Kim is, even her breasts was smaller when she first made her claim into fame. Then I would work my way kissing and licking your stomach and the button on your belly; by then, you wouldn't have much of a problem climaxing after I lick on your other love button and manually stimulate the area a little lower that is as juicy, sticky and wet as jelly. So by the time that I become a plumber and lay some pipe, baby, try not to scream and moan so loud that the neighbors think that we are having a fight; when your stuff starts smacking or queefing, like it's talking to me and telling me how good it is, I know for sure that I am doing it right. When your orgasms come, that's the explosions after the detonation; I'm so glad that the neighbors don't appear to hear it or complain because we would be arrested for disturbing the peace and put on probation. Try not to fall asleep yet, baby, because the match is not done; we have many more rounds to go and that was just Round One.

Separated But Not Sexually Segregated

If you believe that I might be interested in seeing other females now that we are separated, I don't know what you're talking about; when other females try to get next to me, I tell them that I still love my old girl and, for now, to find a new route. Although we are separated, I don't want the little love and passion that we do have for each other to become a drought; I don't want my manly nature and testis to become swollen and enlarged, like they have the gout, so therefore, I want to release all that built up pressure on only you and let all my stored up love and passion for you come flowing out. Make love to me, play with my body and do as you may; just don't play around with my dookie-hole because I will get no pleasure from it since I am not bi-sexual or gay. I want to love you down all over, baby, what do you *say*? I want to show you love and give you some loving and romancing now because I don't want to show you just on Valentine's Day; as long as we maintain the love for each other, you will continue to spontaneously receive gifts from me any day, anyway. Your body continually turn me on, like a light in the darkness, and I want you to relax on me, naked with your clothes gone; I love it when your body calls me, like a telephone and my special love liquid oozes out of my body from my organ into your special holding tank and causes you to scream with pleasure and moan. If I am going to love you, I am going to love you right, anyway and anywhere you like, day or night;

117

I will kiss, suck and nibble on your body because I want to give you total pleasure and not pain so therefore, I will not bite. Lie back and relax so that the ecstatic feeling will be to be the max; I will start out nice and slow but will speed it up little by little as you build up to a climax. I want to continually switch positions, with me on top, you riding me and then I'll flip you over; I want you to then get on your hands and knees as you bend over so that I can get it from the back, doggy style, but just don't be sarcastic and say, "That's a good boy, Rover!" You may think that I am crazy and wild when I do the freaky and exotic things that I do to you; you may think that I am off the chain but, in actuality and reality, your mom and dad, preachers, deacons and church members, doctors, lawyers, dentists, teachers, politicians, etc. may do more stuff than us that's really even more taboo when they get behind closed doors, too. So never feel embarrassed or ashamed when I make your body feel so good that you scream my name; nevertheless, I will put some protection on my erection whenever I show you intimate affection so that, if you end up pregnant, I won't be the only one to blame.

Only You Is Who I Want To Give My Love and Passion To

Baby, the love and passion between us is growing a little cold so allow me to rekindle the fire; let us kiss and suck on each other's bodies, making us less tense and leaving evidence, like a vampire. I want to take all the time that I need to give us total satisfaction, all night long, so use my body as freely as you want and need because I am not for hire; I know that I will get you as hot as an electrical wire and as soaking wet as you make me when I heavily perspire. Whenever you are ready, I will make sweet love to you and try to keep my climaxes and your orgasms steady; afterwards, I will hold you tight, for the remainder of the night, and you can hold and squeeze me with love, as you would a special and favorite teddy. I will never be a menace to you, your life and dreams, like Jason and Freddy; when things go wrong, I will never do crazy things to get back at you because that would be too immature and petty. I will always work hard with you to help you achieve anything positive that your heart, mind and body may desire; as I get older, I will do the same and never change, even after I retire. My passion will be reserved only for you because it is only your heart, mind and body that I want to please; you will never know of me messing around all over town because I want you to burn, sensually, from me with sweet passion and never a venereal disease or scratching continuously, like a clean house dog that has gone out and has gotten the mange and some fleas. And don't mess around on me either because I love the firework show that we shoot off and display after bare *penetration*. If you haven't noticed the fullness of the excitement and thrill, next time we make love, I'll show you a full illustration and demonstration; not only do I have to satisfy your body, in the bedroom or wherever, but also have to satisfy your heart and mind because, as your man, that's my obligation. Tell me what you want and desire of me, as I will tell you, so that we will never have to go looking for those things from another; I don't want to go deep-sea fishing with my pole, in another woman's lake, and it nauseates and sickens me to even think about being with another man packing peanut butter. My passion may not be everlasting but your sex is just so good that, for it, I never want to be fasting; whatever may inhibit us from giving our love and passion to each other to the fullness, those things we have to be getting rid of, quickly, and be trashing. If you want some more of my good loving today, you should come on with it while the getting is good, just like you should; if I could I would give it to you all my life as long and as much as you would want but, as old age comes, it will seem as termites will come to damage and take the life and vitality out of my long, strong and hard wood. Even then, it will be no shame in my game to use Cialis or Viagra; I want to always satisfy you and keep your wetness and juices flowing strongly, like the falls of Niagara.

The Satisfaction Of
Your Love And Passion

Just imagine a cool, warm breeze softly caressing your face and hair; it will be caressing and touching you, intimately, as if it truly cares but, as you open your eyes, you will see only me standing there. I will whisper sweet things in your ear with complete charm and honesty, not just ear candy; if you want to do the same thing or more to me, that's just fine and dandy. I like when you talk dirty and freaky to me, as we prepare to get it on; we don't need anything to inhibit us or slow us down so ease your mind, lock the doors, hide the remotes and do away with the phones with the loud ringing and ring tones. I can't wait to hear you moan, after we finish the foreplay and you *mequito calzones*; you give me so much pleasure and passion with pure love that I can't leave you alone. One day without your loving feels like a week; I want to make sweet love to you so good that during and shortly afterwards, you can barely speak. I want us to satisfy each other to the fullness, completely, because we are each other's personal freak; I don't want us to stop until we both reach one climax or more, as you leak and I skeet. Afterwards, we can have a restful sleep; I have to keep my head together and hold back on how I truly feel because my emotions are getting too deep. I want to pull many more all-night love-making sessions, I am not going to lie; there are many new positions that I want us to try and I'll keep the KY Jelly handy for whenever you start to get too dry.

Whenever you don't feel like making love, you don't have to use "having a headache" or "being on your "menstruation" as an alibi; you can simply tell me that you don't feel like doing it at the time and I won't even try. I will simply snuggle and hold you with my embrace, in the bed; I have no problem talking with you about our feelings for each other, how our day has been or reminiscing on sweeter moments that we shared with each other in the past, instead. The reasons that I really, truly love you don't involve *sex*. When things go wrong, I never have to wreck my brain struggling on what to do next; the way that I feel and the things that I do to please you are so true, natural and real and can never be taught in any school text. You can always come to me, freely, whenever you need love and passion; my love, passion, care, respect, appreciation, honesty, faithfulness, etc., will never be expended so there's no need at all to ration. I am never content, until we both receive full satisfaction; I get tired of only telling you what I want to do to you before we make love because I am more of a man of action. I refuse to stop, until I get the job done; I just wish that my career could be this satisfyingly fun, as exciting as the times that I am with you, so that I can put in work until the rising of the sun. Working on your body never gets boring or dull because it is such an easy task; I am ready to give you pleasure any time that you want it, sometimes before you even can ask.

Printed in the United States
By Bookmasters